P9-CCZ-806

This book belongs to:

_____

www.winslowpress.com

DISCARDED
BY THE
NORRISTOWN PUBLIC LIBRARY

Water Rat

Marnie Laird

Illustrations by
Andrea Shine

WINSLOW PRESS

I wish to gratefully acknowledge
the ongoing encouragement of
Joe Goulden and Robert Robinson.
Additionally, I want to thank Robert's brother,
Tom Robinson,
for his knowledge of nautical details.

J
LAI

To my grandfather, the late Daniel J. Layton,
Chief Justice of Delaware,
who instilled in me as a young girl
a passion for books.

731311

Water Rat

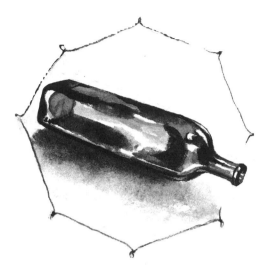

Chapter One

The room smelled
of stale tobacco smoke
and sour wine.

Matt gathered the firewood, taking his time. Eli was in a bad mood, and Matt figured the longer he stayed out of sight, the better. When he had as many logs as he could manage, he paused for a moment, balancing on his good right leg while adjusting his thin body to the weight of the wood. Then he turned and slowly limped back to the tavern.

"Dawdling again? You good-for-nothing! Where've you been?" Eli demanded as Matt entered the tavern. He glared at Matt out of small, bloodshot eyes. An open jug of rum stood on the counter next to him. When Eli got into the rum this early in the day, it was a bad sign. Matt knew he was in for trouble and tried to avoid Eli's stare.

"Here I am, feeding you, putting a roof over your head, and what do I get for it?" Eli shouted, slamming his fist on the counter so hard that several mugs clinked together. "Well, I'll tell you what I've got! A fourteen-year-old—without home nor kin to call his own—who don't think he's got to work for his keep!"

Matt felt the old familiar fear stirring in the pit of his stomach, twisting and turning, sending little tremors he couldn't control through his body. He looked away from Eli's red, surly face and headed toward the fireplace on the other side of the room.

"Dang you, boy! Are you deaf as well as lame? Answer me when I speak!" Eli took another swig of rum and belched.

Matt cursed the fear that was paralyzing him so much that he couldn't think straight. He heard Eli move from behind the bar. At the same moment, Matt stumbled over a chair leg and fell forward. The logs spilled, rolling helter-skelter across the floor. The fall knocked the wind out of him and he lay still, trying to catch his breath.

In a flash, Eli was at his side. Matt knew what was coming next. Out of the corner of his eye, he saw the upraised boot and desperately tried to roll out of the way.

The heavy boot glanced off his side. He gasped with pain.

"Get up, you clumsy oaf!" Eli shouted and stomped out to the back room that served as the tavern's kitchen.

Matt lay still, biting his lip to keep from crying out—that would only mean more trouble, and trouble was something he wanted to avoid. Instead, he let his hatred of Eli flood through him and wished Eli dead, as he had so many times in the four years since Pa died. Self-pity joined forces with the hatred, adding to his misery. I'm nothing but a slave here, he thought bitterly.

Gradually, the pain eased, and Matt slowly got to his feet. At least he'd missed the worst of the kick. He bent over to pick up the scattered firewood.

When he had the wood stacked by the hearth, Matt got a broom and swept the wide-pegged floors. He looked around the room. The whitewashed walls were grimy, and smoke had darkened the paneling around the fireplace. Several chairs had been turned over during last night's carousing, and a table in the corner was missing a leg.

A rough group of men, trappers from up around Appoquinimink, had entered the tavern early in the evening, looking for food and drink. Matt had served them, fetching bottles of whiskey and refilling plates, keeping out of their way as much as possible. Later, back in the tiny lean-to that he shared with bits and pieces of tavern equipment, he had tossed and turned on his bare mattress, kept awake by the shouts and singing in the tavern.

Signs of last night's activities were still around the room. Empty wine bottles and dirty pewter plates littered the long tavern table. A platter holding a knife and the remains of a round of cheese sat in the center. The candles had burned down, their dribbles of wax hardened on the table. The room smelled of stale tobacco smoke and sour wine.

Matt started clearing the table. He gathered a load of dirty dishes and carried them out into the kitchen. Eli was carving a ham as if nothing had happened. Matt hurried back and forth between the barroom and kitchen, avoiding Eli as much as possible.

Within a short time, lunch customers started dropping in. Matt sliced some thick, crusty bread, put it on a platter along with the ham and remaining cheese, and carried it out to the table. Several men lounged against the bar, where Eli was pouring drinks. Scraps of conversation floated above the background noise of chairs scraping the pegged floor and the clatter of plates.

"Nice weather, warm for April," a bearded waterman remarked.

"About time," a trapper replied. "People say this winter of 1748 will go down in history, and I believe it. Why, in February, when I was up in New Castle, the Delaware River froze solid overnight. I saw a herd of deer crossing from our shores to the Jersey side."

"That is hard to believe," the waterman said. "Though, I grant you, it was the coldest winter I've known." He shoved his tankard toward Eli for a refill.

"Don't blame you for doubting it," the trapper agreed. "Even the Indians who still live here in the Lower Counties couldn't remember that happening before." He finished his drink, threw a coin on the bar, and departed.

While Matt was in the kitchen getting more bread, Mingo came through the back door, stopping first to scrape the mud off his boots.

"What's wrong with you, boy?" he asked, removing his cap.

Matt didn't answer, but he knew what the black man meant. Matt had never been able to hide his feelings.

"Boy, you and me, we don't have too many good times around here, do we?" Mingo continued.

"Eli's drinkin'," Matt blurted out. "I tripped and fell down and he kicked me—hard as he could. Seems like he gets a real pleasure from beatin' on me."

Mingo looked at him sadly. "Too bad you and me can't switch jobs—you do the outside work and me do the inside. Maybe Eli wouldn't pick on a growed man so much."

"Someday maybe I won't be here fer him to beat on no more," Matt said grimly.

"What stuff you talkin' 'bout?" Mingo demanded, looking at Matt intently.

"Just what I said," replied Matt, wiping his nose with the back of his sleeve. "Who says I've got to stay here? He don't own me!" He spat on the floor for emphasis.

"Where you fixin' on goin'?" Mingo asked. "You don't got money or folks, you don't got a trade, and you don't got nowheres to go. You'll find yourself in a heap more trouble than you got 'round here. At least here, you got food in your gut and a roof over your head."

"Maybe I'll just have to find out fer myself!" Matt said.

"I tries to make the best of things," Mingo said. "A slave don't got much choice. But you—you're still a young'un. Maybe when you're growed some more, you'll find a better place."

How, with this leg? Matt thought bitterly. Who would hire me?

After the customers had left and the tables were cleared, Eli told Mingo and Matt to change the candles in the pewter disks hanging from the ceiling. "I'm going out," he added.

Shortly afterward, when Matt was steadying the ladder for Mingo, a stranger suddenly appeared in the bar. His face was red, as if he were used to living outdoors, and a thin, wispy mustache drooped down either side of his mouth.

"Where's Eli?" he asked, his glance darting nervously around the room. Mingo, who hadn't noticed him, was so startled at the strange voice that he almost fell off the ladder.

Matt stared at the man, feeling a flicker of distrust at his manner and at the way he had sneaked in the back door as silently as a snake slips through tall grass.

"Can I git you somethin'?" Matt asked.

"Ale," the man said. Glancing around the room, he chose a table in the corner, farthest from the front door.

While Matt was behind the bar drawing the ale, Eli strode into the room and saw the stranger. Matt spotted the look the two men exchanged.

"I've come on business," the man said quietly to Eli.

Eli's eyes narrowed and he said quickly, "Mingo, get down from there. You and Matt take the rest of the day off. I won't need you 'til nightfall."

Chapter Two

Matt headed for the bank,
figuring he could always pole the
skiff along its edge and be safe.

Matt shut the door, glad to leave the dingy tavern behind. He stopped for a moment to enjoy the April sunshine. Across the dirt road, the narrow Leipsic River wound through the marshes that stretched into the distance as far as he could see. He watched gulls, coasting on air currents, scanning the marshes for food. Here and there, faint touches of green signaled that spring was on its way.

Mingo came around the corner of the tavern.

"Can you help me git my skiff out?" Matt asked him. "I'm goin' fishin'. Want to come?"

"No thanks, boy. I'm goin' over to Sherburn to see Bessie," Mingo replied.

Between them, they hauled the boat out of the shed by the dock and slowly eased it down the muddy bank. It landed in the river with a splash that sent ripples chasing across the water.

"That sure's a puzzle, us gettin' the afternoon off like that," said Mingo.

"Eli knew that man," Matt said. "I saw the way they looked at each other."

"Well, I never seen him 'fore. He looked sly, like a fox," Mingo stated.

Matt was too busy getting the boat ready to give much thought to the stranger. He laid the oars and fishing gear in the bottom and stepped into the boat, balancing carefully as it tilted under his weight. After he was settled, he inserted the oarlocks and slid the oars into place. Using the long pole he kept in the boat, Matt shoved off from the bank.

On Matt's right, the great salt marsh extended eastward until, eventually, it merged into the deep waters of the Delaware Bay. Only the faint pencil-like strokes of bare trees against the blue sky marked the distant horizon. Hummocks—high patches of ground on which pines and scrub grew—dotted the area. A whole network of creeks, some narrow, others wide enough for fair-sized boats, cut through the landscape.

"Ahoy, there!" a man shouted. A small sloop, carrying a family toward Fast Landing, was approaching on his port side. Matt waved and navigated the skiff out of its way.

He decided to head downstream, where the fishing should be good this time of year. The wind would be behind him going down, and the incoming tide would help coming back. The pain in his side forgotten, Matt leaned into the oars and rounded the wooded point that protected the western edge of the harbor.

Out in the river, Matt smelled the sharp odor of the marshes, a mixture of salt air, rich, oozing mud, and dank marsh grass. Little waves slapped at the bow of his boat. Ahead of him, a muskrat slipped down the bank and swam away.

Getting the whole afternoon off was a stroke of luck, and Matt, like Mingo, wondered at Eli's generosity. Whatever it was, it had something to do with the mysterious stranger. The river bent to his right after he passed the entrance to Broad Creek.

"Look! There's a rat! A real-live rat!" Voices and laughter carried clearly across the water.

Matt jerked around. Two boys about his age were standing on a dock pointing and laughing at him. With a sinking feeling, Matt ducked his head and hunched his bony shoulders as if he could disappear, turtle-like, into his own shell.

"You mean the Water Rat, don't you?" shouted the other one. "The boy who won't speak to people and who creeps around the marsh—just like the rest of the muskrats."

Matt winced as the first boy guffawed. How could he make friends when he worked in a tavern? He glared resentfully at the two boys. They had homes and decent clothes to wear. They didn't have to work from dawn until way past nightfall.

He dug the oars into the water. His only friends were Mingo and Quinn, the Indian who lived in an old shack hidden on the marsh. If only Quinn would let him stay at his place! Eli could never find him there, but so far the Indian had refused. Mingo was right—there was nowhere for him to go. Miserable, Matt leaned over the oars, rowing with all his strength. As the boat gained speed, the boys receded into the distance until they were no more than dots silhouetted against the shoreline.

The wind picked up, and small whitecaps flecked the water. After a bit, Matt's boat passed Campbell's Creek. He couldn't see the Campbell house from the river because of the woods, but he remembered the time when he and his father had taken the skiff down the creek. Pa had pointed out the brick house sitting on a rise, back from the water's edge.

"That's Journey's End, Doc Campbell's place," Pa had told him, spitting a stream of tobacco juice over the boat's side. "His old man got about five hundred acres of good farm land from the Indians by bartering glass beads and other junk. Doc, he sold some, but he's still got a right nice-sized place."

The river was widening now. When Matt came to Herring Creek on his right, he nosed the skiff into its entrance. Just inside the mouth of the creek was a twisted pine with several large branches leaning over the left bank. Once or twice, on blistering hot summer days, Matt had poled under the shelter of its overhanging branches and fished. But today was cold, so he kept on rowing.

He had never been this far down the creek before; Quinn had warned him the channel was silted in. A pool of water lay around the next bend, and Matt dropped anchor in the middle. He rolled some bread into balls, baited his line, and settled himself comfortably, letting the stillness and the April sunshine wash over him. Eli and the tavern seemed in another, faraway world.

Matt had a couple of nibbles before he felt a solid jerk. When he hauled the fish into the boat, he saw it was a good-sized shad. Maybe Eli would let him cook it for supper instead of salting it and putting it away for a special customer.

When the sun disappeared, Matt shivered and buttoned his worn cloth jacket. The sleeves left several inches of forearm showing. Tall plumes of marsh grass, lining the creek banks, blocked the horizon so that, at first, he didn't notice the fog drifting in from the bay. But when he stood up in the boat to toss his line out again, he saw a wall of gray, billowy clouds rolling toward him across the marsh.

Matt threw together his gear, raised anchor, and rowed toward the creek mouth as fast as he could. It was dangerous to be alone in a boat in a thick fog. At first, it was a heavy haze, but soon the fog swirled around him, cold and damp, deadening the marsh sounds and hiding familiar landmarks.

Matt headed for the bank, figuring he could always pole the skiff along its edge and be safe. It was something Pa had taught him. "Keep your head and keep close to the bank," Pa used to say. Matt soon settled into a steady rhythm, first leaning forward over the bow to push the heavy pole down to the creek bottom, then slowly straightening his wiry body as he pulled against the pole to move the skiff another couple of yards along the shoreline. It was slow work against the incoming tide, but following the bank would lead him to the river. Once there, the incoming tide would help carry him back to Fast Landing. Still, his heart pounded at the thought of becoming stranded alone in the marsh.

Matt paused and peered about. He couldn't see beyond the bow. No matter which way he looked, it was the same: soft, white drifting veils of fog, eddying on invisible currents over the creek and marsh. He gripped the pole tighter and kept working along the bank. The fog lifted for a second, revealing shadowy outlines of trees before descending again and closing him in its silent, blind world.

Finally, up ahead, Matt caught a glimpse of something dark outlined against the white. Poling closer, he saw it was the old pine with the twisted branches—that meant he was almost back at the river. He stopped under the overhanging branches to rest. The fog pressed down, silent and heavy, blotting out the landscape in all directions. Matt shivered in the dampness and pulled the jacket collar up around his neck.

Suddenly, the stillness was broken by a gurgling sound. Matt dropped his hands and listened. He heard splashing followed by creaking sounds. Something big, very big, was moving through the water toward him. As he peered through the branches in the direction of the sound, Matt froze. Through the swirling fog, he saw the long, low outline of a large ship. He leaned forward to get a better look. From behind the screen of the low-hanging pine boughs, Matt watched as the ship slowly glided past, its wake violently rocking his skiff. In another moment, it disappeared, swallowed by the fog. Other than the bow cutting through the water and the creaking mast, there hadn't been a sound: no voices, no bells, no nothing. Matt felt prickles on the back of his neck. It was as though a ghost ship, sailed by ghosts of men, had been close enough for him to reach out and touch.

The ship carried a couple of jibs on a very long bowsprit and a large mainsail on a single, tall mast. Other than that, nothing, not even an identifying flag. Matt let out his breath and rubbed his eyes. All he could see was swirling fog; the ship had disappeared without a trace. In spite of Mingo's tales, Matt didn't believe in ghosts. Besides, the skiff was still rocking in the ship's wake.

What kind of ship was she, he wondered, and where were the men who sailed her? Matt grabbed the oars. Ducking under the pine boughs, he blindly headed out of the creek's mouth into the river and rowed as hard as he could for the opposite shore.

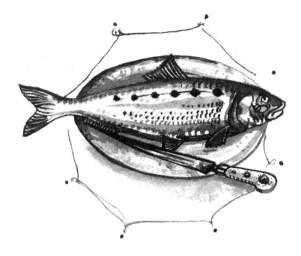

Chapter Three

He laid the fish on the
kitchen table and hung his jacket
on a wooden peg. Just then, Eli
came through the door.

It was dark when Matt got back. Eli would be furious that he was so late. As he trudged up the slope from the river, he saw Mingo lighting the candles in the tavern windows. He hurried around to the rear, hoping to sneak in unnoticed.

The kitchen felt warm to Matt after he had been out on the river. He laid the fish on the kitchen table and hung his jacket on a wooden peg. Just then, Eli came through the door. Matt caught his breath.

"See you didn't come back empty handed," Eli remarked.

Matt relaxed. Maybe it was going to be all right after all. "I caught a big shad," he answered slowly.

"Got caught in the fog too, didn't you?" Eli asked.

Matt kept quiet, not knowing what to say.

"Well, customers ain't going to be dropping in on a night like this. Couldn't find their way through this pea soup at any rate," Eli laughed. It wasn't a pleasant sound. Long ago, Matt had noticed that when Eli laughed or smiled, his eyes remained watchful and mean.

"I'm thinking fresh shad would make a good supper tonight," Eli added.

Matt was astonished. He looked questioningly at the big man. Eli sniggered and returned to the bar. Matt took the fish to the wooden table and filleted it. Throwing another log on the kitchen fire, he placed the fillets and a knob of butter in a large black iron skillet to cook them. After a while, Mingo came into the kitchen.

"You had luck today," he said.

"More than that," Matt replied.

"What do you mean?" Mingo asked as Eli returned to the kitchen. Matt fell silent and bent over the fire, carefully turning the shad. In a few minutes, the fish was done. Matt slid it onto a platter, pouring the juices over it.

"Nothing like fresh shad after a long winter," Eli said, sitting down at the rough plank table. He wiped his dirty hands on the filthy apron tied at his waist. The fish was tender and moist, a welcome treat after the stews they'd eaten all winter. Eli ate greedily, shoving fish and potatoes into his mouth. With the back of his hairy hand, he wiped away the rivulets of melted butter that ran down his stubbled chin.

After dinner, Eli mumbled something about checking the root cellar and disappeared down the rickety steps. Neither Mingo nor Matt had ever been allowed in the storeroom, although they both knew that that was where the whiskey was kept. Mingo went outside and brought in a pail of water from the well, for washing up.

"Master sure seems in a good mood tonight," he commented.

Matt could hear Eli rummaging around below. "Mingo, I seen somethin' today," he whispered as he swished the water and lye soap over the pewter plates. "A strange ship down near the bay. It come into Herrin' Crick just as I was gittin' set to row out into the river."

"What'd it look like?" Mingo asked.

"Not like any ship I seen before," replied Matt. He described the ship to Mingo, who listened intently.

"A long bowsprit but only one mainsail, you say?" repeated Mingo. "There's no ship like that I've heard tell of."

"But that's not all," Matt went on, shifting his weight onto his good leg and leaning against the sink. "There weren't no sailors. Leastways, none I seen nor heard. The ship sailed by me with nary a sound. No flags neither." Matt turned a troubled face toward the black man.

"You seen the ghost ship!" Mingo exclaimed.

Matt felt a clutch of fear in the pit of his stomach. "What ship's that?" he asked.

"The one that sailed into Little Crick with the captain's body hanging from the bowsprit," Mingo answered.

"What happened?" Matt asked. In spite of himself, he wanted to hear more.

"Folks say the captain wanted to marry a girl livin' near

Little Crick, but on the trip home he done found out that his first lieutenant was in love with her too. They had a duel and the captain, he lost. The lieutenant strung up his body."

"Did the lieutenant marry the girl?"

"She wouldn't have him after that. Ended up marrying someone else. Or so they say. Folks swear they seen his ship cruising close to shore when there's a heavy fog."

Matt stared at Mingo. Was it the ghost ship that he'd seen? The ship had certainly seemed deserted. The thought sent shivers up his spine. He glanced out the window. Fog pressed against the darkened panes. He turned back to Mingo.

"Ghosts ain't real," he said in a quavering voice.

Mingo was quiet for a moment. The candlelight showed the serious expression on his face. "Best not to say a word 'bout this, boy," he cautioned, laying a friendly hand on Matt's shoulder. "Folks like us do well to keep quiet. Understand?" He nervously fingered the herb-filled red-flannel amulet he wore around his neck for good luck.

As Matt digested Mingo's information, a door slammed in the cellar. Eli started up the stairs, whistling. Matt returned to the dishes. Mingo took a lantern and left for the barn, where he slept on a pallet in an empty stall.

Chapter Four

Matt turned and headed
for the general store around
the next bend.

One morning in May, Eli called Matt into the tavern early. "Git me three dozen candles. Be sure they're the long ones. And bring back some salt, ten pounds of flour, and a round of cheese. Got that?"

Matt repeated the list.

"Tell ol' man Hazard to put it on my account, and don't forget nothin' or I'll see you're sorry." He gave Matt a shove that sent him stumbling out the door.

Matt was secretly delighted. The day was bright and sunny, a sharp contrast to the gloomy tavern. His worn shoes pinched his feet. He took them off and tucked them under a bush near the tavern door.

Matt limped down the road, enjoying the feel of the warm earth under his bare feet. The wind blew off the water, gusting now and then, sending little swirls of dust skittering across the road. Out on the river, some men were angling their sloop toward Fast Landing.

Matt rounded the bend and saw the village up ahead. Small frame houses with picket fences lined both sides of the road. In several yards, muskrat skins, stretched tightly on pointed shingles, were drying in the sun. They would be sold to the fur traders who visited the village. Matt quickened his step at the sight of the unusual number of boats anchored at the wharf.

Men crowded the dock, jostling each other as they struggled to see the cargo each boat carried. Sails snapped and billowed in the breeze, while gulls shrieked, waiting for handouts. Good-natured shouts rang out from the crews of the different boats. Matt made his way through the crowd, carefully studying each of the ships. None resembled the mysterious boat that had passed him in Herring Creek last month.

"Watch out, lad!" shouted a burly man dragging a large cage containing snapping turtles down the dock. Matt jumped out of his way.

Sailors unloaded cargoes of shad, sturgeon, trout, and

perch that glistened in the sunlight. Two bearded men tossed a net holding a huge eel, thick as a man's forearm, onto the dock. Matt watched the eel twist and hiss at its captors. Then Matt looked over the marshes. The tide was running out, and the vast, muddy, wet flats followed the river's curve. The wind had picked up, bringing the salty smell of the sea inland.

Matt turned and headed for the general store around the next bend. A horse and carriage were tied to the railing outside. He entered quietly and stood still for a moment, absorbing spicy scents of ginger, nutmeg, cloves, and mace mixed with the salty odor of the hams and sides of bacon hanging from the rafters. Dried apples, sugar, tea, and the bittersweet scent of molasses fused with the rich, leathery smell of harnesses.

At the counter, a small woman was asking Mr. Hazard for some calico. Matt looked at the shelves laden with bolts of homespun, linen, and spools of brightly colored thread. On another side, shelves displayed dusty bottles, stoneware jugs, and candles. There were ropes, penknives, fishing line, hooks, and sinkers. Fishnets dangled from the ceiling. Barrels filled with seed, flour, and hogs' lard sprouted like toadstools from the dusty floor.

The woman's voice interrupted Matt's thoughts.

"Mr. Hazard, have you gotten the ribbons I've been wanting for my girls?"

"No, Mrs. Campbell. This bloody war is causing me all kinds of trouble."

"When England is fighting France, it's hard to believe it could interfere with life on the other side of the Atlantic," she replied.

The storekeeper peered at her over the top of his spectacles. "It interferes with our lives because England took away the warships that were guarding our coast. We're England's Crown Colony, but that doesn't count for much when they need ships for their wars overseas. Since then, outside some of the big ports like New York and Philadelphia, pirates have gotten bolder, interfering with shipping. And when that happens, supplies don't get through. It's a bad situation. Now, ma'am, anything else you need?"

Matt studied the woman with interest. She must be the wife of the doctor who lived in the big house that Pa had pointed out.

"I need some sugar and a pair of scissors, besides the calico. Oh, and a pound of tea, if you please."

Matt watched as the storekeeper collected the items and as she paid him.

"Excuse me," Mrs. Campbell said, smiling at Matt as she passed him in the aisle on her way out.

Matt approached the counter, repeating to himself Eli's list: candles, flour, salt, and cheese. Mr. Hazard nodded at him. "Hello, young Matt. Take your time. I'll be back in a minute," he said, disappearing into the rear annex.

Matt was counting the candles when he heard a scream. Jerking around, he saw Mrs. Campbell clinging to her carriage seat. The horse was on its hind legs, pawing the air with its hooves. Packages spilled onto the ground. The horse neighed shrilly and pulled backward. Any moment, its rope might snap, Matt realized. He dropped the candles and rushed outside. The horse plunged in its traces, throwing its head and rolling its eyes. Mrs. Campbell clung to her seat, white faced.

Matt grabbed for the bridle and missed. Once again the horse reared, neighed loudly, and pulled backward. Mrs. Campbell screamed. There wasn't time to think. When the horse came down, Matt lunged for its head and grabbed the bridle firmly with both hands. The horse threw its head wildly, pulling him first in one direction, then another. Matt closed his eyes and hung on with all his strength. Flecks of foam from the horse's mouth spattered over him. He didn't know how long he'd be able to keep his grip.

"Sam! Help! Sam!" Mrs. Campbell cried.

Matt opened his eyes just in time to see a short black man grab the bridle on the other side of the horse.

"Whoa, boy. Easy. Take it easy," Sam said again and again.

"Don't let go!" Mrs. Campbell begged.

Matt felt the horse trembling violently. "Whoa, boy," he said, following Sam's example. He stroked its quivering neck. Gradually, the horse calmed down. Matt gathered up the reins and looked at Mrs. Campbell.

"Oh, thank heavens!" she exclaimed. "How fortunate you were here! If you hadn't come along, I'm sure he would have bolted." She straightened up in the seat. Her face was pale, and she was breathing rapidly. She turned to Sam. "What happened to you?" she demanded. "You were supposed to be back a while ago."

"Sorry, missus," he apologized. "But I wuz waitin' at the weaver's for the doctor's material."

"If it weren't for this boy, I could have been killed!" she persisted vehemently. "Loose newspaper blew down the street and spooked the horse."

Sam looked embarrassed. "Doc says I wuz to make sure and bring the material back," he said again, handing her the packages that had fallen on the ground.

Matt stood awkwardly, balancing on his right leg, holding on to the reins. Mrs. Campbell turned to him.

"What's your name?" she asked.

"Matt. Matt Burton, ma'am," he answered, avoiding her eyes.

"Where do you live?"

"Down the road a bit," he replied, ashamed to admit he lived in a tavern.

"Who are your parents?" she asked. "I must tell them what a fine thing you've done today."

There was no way out of it. "I live in Eli's tavern," he stated defiantly, looking directly at her. "I've got no folks. They're dead."

"I see," she murmured. "How old are you, Matt?"

"Fourteen, this winter."

The carriage tilted as Sam climbed in. Mrs. Campbell looked down at Matt.

"I'm Mrs. Campbell, the surgeon's wife," she said. "We live out at Journey's End on a waterway my father-in-law named Campbell's Creek. I owe you a great debt for what you did for me today. If there ever comes a time when either my husband or I can help you in any way, you know where to find us." Matt could tell she was serious.

"T'weren't nothin', ma'am," Matt mumbled.

"Indeed it was! You saved me from a dreadful accident. Now, remember—Journey's End on Campbell's Creek. I mean what I say." She smiled.

Sam clucked to the horse, and the carriage started slowly down the road. Suddenly, three boys ran around the corner across the street.

"Rat! Water Rat!" the tallest one jeered. "Hey, what do you think you're doing in town? You belong in the marshes!" All three guffawed. Matt stood rooted to the road. His gaze followed the carriage. Sure enough, Mrs. Campbell had heard. She turned in her seat and looked back at him.

Three against one. There was no way he could fight them. Glaring at the boys, Matt straightened his shoulders and limped back into the store.

Chapter Five

"When the Shawnee left this area,
taking with them the bones of our
ancestors, it was to find a new home."

Drat you, boy! Where are you?"
Matt stopped sweeping, propped the broom against a table, and limped to the kitchen. Twice recently, Eli had beaten him badly, once for moving slowly and the second time for spilling water in the kitchen. He saw immediately that Eli was drunk. Cupboard doors were askew, the lids of several tins lay scattered on the counter, and a stool was overturned.

"I've got a hankering for fresh fish. Take your skiff and go catch me some!" Eli ordered, his voice thick.

"You told me to sweep the tavern," Matt reminded him.

"Don't argue!" Eli shouted, raising his fist. Matt jumped out of the way.

"All right," Matt agreed quickly. Taking care to stay out of Eli's reach, he grabbed some bread and scurried out.

It was a still day and unusually warm for mid-May. Trees were sporting little green umbrellas of spring leaves. Once out on the water, Matt kept a sharp eye out for any strange ships as he rowed, but there were few boats on the river.

When he came to Indian Gut, a twisting waterway stretching to the back reaches of the marsh where Quinn lived, Matt decided, on an impulse, to see if his friend was home. The Indian knew everything that happened in the marshes, and he might know something about the boat that had sneaked into Herring Creek, Matt figured. Unless, of course, Mingo was right and it really was a ghost ship. The thought again sent shivers up Matt's spine.

It was even warmer in the protection of the gut, and Matt began to sweat. Ahead of him, the stick-like figure of a crane lifted gracefully from the bank and, flapping its wings, headed silently toward the river. The marshes stretched for miles, green, shimmering in the sun, edged along the horizon by a backdrop of dark pines. The gut narrowed as Matt neared Quinn's shack, and Matt poled the remaining distance. Then he spotted the Indian's dugout, concealed among the thick reeds lining the bank.

Matt threaded his way quietly up the overgrown path, hoping to surprise Quinn, but the thatch-roofed, ramshackle hut was empty. Matt circled the shack, but there were no signs of Quinn in the surrounding glade of scrub oak. Disappointed, Matt returned to the path that led to the water. Halfway down, he heard an owl hoot. The sound came from a nearby clump of trees. Matt raised his head but couldn't spot the owl. When Matt looked again, Quinn was standing in front of him, blocking the path.

"Where'd you come from?" Matt asked, startled.

"I was here," the Indian replied, a glint of amusement flickering in his eye.

"I was huntin' high and low fer you," Matt said.

Quinn gave a rare smile. "The white man is different from the Indian. I can travel on wings of air so that even the birds and squirrels don't give me away." He slapped irritably at a bug. "Come inside, away from the flies, and we will talk."

Matt followed Quinn up the path. He bent low to enter the Indian's hut. Inside it was dark and musty smelling. A heap of tattered blankets lay in a corner on the hard-packed dirt floor; dried herbs hung from a ceiling beam. A circle of flat stones and several inches of ash marked where Quinn cooked.

"Sit!" the Indian commanded, lowering his own lean body to the ground. "Do you think Quinn doesn't know everything that goes on in the marshes?" he asked. "This morning I am in my garden and I see the great heron leave his fishing spot and fly across the marsh. It was early for him to stop feeding. Then I hear the gulls screeching, so I go to the top of the path and I see you, poling down the gut. So I decided to hide and surprise my friend."

Quinn got up, searched around in a dark corner, and returned with his clay pipe. After he lit it, he looked at Matt. "Why did you come today?" he asked.

"Eli," Matt said. "He's bin beatin' on me again. I wish

you'd let me stay here, Quinn. I'd do what you say!" he finished in a burst.

The Indian frowned. "We have talked about this before. You are my friend, but if we both lived here, maybe we wouldn't be friends for long. I have lived alone a long while. It would not work to have you here all the time. Better to leave things the way they are."

Matt sighed. There was no arguing with Quinn.

"Besides," the Indian continued, "sometimes I think I will follow my people who left to go west six years ago."

A pang shot through Matt. "You mean you'd leave here? Fer good?" If Quinn left, it would be terrible.

The Indian puffed on his pipe before continuing. "When the Shawnee left this area, taking with them the bones of our ancestors, it was to find a new home. Most of the land here, where we have hunted and fished since the time my memory begins, has been claimed by the white man."

"You told me you didn't go west 'cause you loved it here," Matt protested.

"That is so," the Indian replied. "In my heart, this is my home. But things change—even here in the marsh." He puffed at his pipe, a faraway look in his eyes.

Matt shifted. "I had another reason fer comin' today, Quinn," he said. "Have you seen a strange ship in the marsh? One with a couple of jibs on a long bowsprit but only one mainsail?"

Quinn stared at him, his gaze intent.

"I seen it in Herrin' Crick 'bout a month ago—"

"Herring Creek!" the Indian interrupted. "I told you to stay away from there!"

"I didn't go in far," Matt said. "The ship passed me near the entrance. It was headed down the crick. Have you seen it?"

Quinn said nothing. He stared ahead, puffs of smoke rising from his pipe. Matt asked the question again, but the Indian remained silent.

"Mingo says it was the ghost ship," Matt continued. "Do you believe in ghosts, Quinn?"

The Indian took the pipe from his mouth. "I believe in what I see with my own eyes," he finally replied.

"Mingo says folks see it on foggy nights, and it sure was foggy when I seen it."

"You were foolish to be out in the fog alone," Quinn said sternly. "The marsh is dangerous." His eyes were fixed on a spot somewhere behind Matt.

"I kin take care of myself in the marsh!" Matt asserted. He paused. "Did you see the boat I'm talkin' 'bout? Did you?"

The Indian had lapsed into silence. Finally, Matt rose to his feet. "I've got to go," he said.

Quinn stood up. "I will walk with you to your boat."

They had almost reached the water when the Indian grabbed Matt's arm. "Look!" he said, pointing skyward.

Matt followed the direction in which the Indian was pointing. An eagle was soaring across the marsh, balancing its huge wings on the air currents.

"The eagle is a friend of my people," Quinn explained. "When the Great Spirit calls, it is the eagle that carries the soul up to the heavens."

Matt climbed into the skiff and pushed off. Suddenly he remembered an old saying: "And he shall raise you up on the wings of eagles." Where had he heard that, Matt pondered as he began poling. Then it came back to him: he had heard it long ago, when his mother used to read the Bible aloud in the evening.

"Good-bye, Quinn," he called. But the Indian was silent, watching the eagle's flight.

Chapter Six

Lightning flashed again, and in the
brief second before darkness
returned, Matt saw the skiff tied
at the river's edge.

The afternoon had been overcast and was hot and humid for early June. Looking outside, Matt saw large thunderheads, gray rimmed with white edges, looming to the south. He was in the kitchen starting supper when the bell jingled. Wiping his hands on his pants, Matt limped into the bar. He stopped at the sight of the gentleman standing on the threshold.

The man's tailored blue waistcoat and fitted trousers that tucked into the tops of well-polished boots were a far cry from the rough clothes worn by local customers. His eyes were cold, brown slits in his beefy, red face. "You're open for business, I presume?" the man asked in a haughty voice.

"Yes, sir," Matt said.

"Then fetch me some of your best brandy," he ordered, sitting down at a table and loosening the white cravat around his neck.

Matt found a bottle and poured the drink. He heard Eli come into the kitchen.

"Why ain't you fixing supper?" Eli called.

"I'm waitin' on somebody," Matt replied.

Eli came into the room and stopped for a moment, studying the gentleman. His expression changed. A smile creased his face. "Well, now, what can I do for you, sir?" he asked.

"My name's Barrett," the man said, after a long swallow. "I've been on the road all day and I'd like some dinner."

He gulped down the rest of his drink. "And some more brandy!"

"Right away, sir!" Eli said, looking at Matt. "And we'll fix you a fine supper, too."

Matt went back into the kitchen and started slicing cold leftover chicken. Thunder rumbled in the distance, rattling the windows. He looked outside. Lightning flickered across the sky.

"Boy!" Mr. Barrett called in a voice that brooked no delay. Matt returned to the room. "My horse is tethered outside, and there's a storm coming. Stable him for me."

"Of course," Eli agreed. Turning to Matt, he added, "Put him in one of the empty stalls."

"Wait a moment," Mr. Barrett said. He rose, stepped outside, and returned with a heavy saddlebag slung over one arm.

Matt took the horse around to the barn, unsaddled it, and led it into a stall. Eli's sure bein' nice to that gentleman, he thought. By the time he headed back, the first raindrops were pockmarking the sandy soil.

Mr. Barrett drank steadily all through dinner. Whenever his glass neared empty, Eli hastened to refill it.

"I own a tannery in Wilmington," Mr. Barrett remarked to Eli. "One of the biggest in the Lower Counties," he boasted.

"Is that so?" Eli asked.

"Yes, I'm on a trip down the coast, making arrangements to buy animal skins. I'm meeting my partner in Baltimore and we're going to head west to buy up all the furs we can." His speech was slurred. "Fill my glass up again, innkeeper," he ordered. His face was growing redder.

"Right away, sir," Eli answered. As he returned from filling the glass, he looked at Matt waiting in the kitchen. "I'll take care of the gentleman. You go to bed," Eli ordered.

Matt dashed through the pouring rain to his lean-to, thankful to have been let off early. He curled up on his pallet and closed his eyes.

It was dark when Matt awoke. He had no idea what time it was or what had awakened him. He opened the lean-to door. Outside, it was drizzling; the heavy rain had let up. Light shone from the tavern window. Eli must have forgotten to blow out the candles, Matt thought as he crept barefoot through the wet grass and peered through the window.

Mr. Barrett was slumped over the table. His glass lay on its side, and brandy dripped slowly onto the floor. Matt watched Eli pick up the saddlebag, open it, and feel around inside. Then, with a disgusted look, he placed it over a chair. He then turned and bent over Mr. Barrett. Matt held his breath as he watched Eli carefully search Mr. Barrett's pockets. Mr. Barrett let out a snore. Suddenly, Eli straightened up with a smile. He was clutching a leather pouch.

Eli hurried to another table and sat down. He opened the pouch and emptied its contents into his lap, but not before Matt saw the gleam of gold. Eli carefully counted the coins into neat piles on the table, every now and then casting a glance at Mr. Barrett. Matt had never seen so much money in his life.

Matt ducked his head as Eli rose to his feet. The rain fell harder now, but Matt didn't notice. Lightning flashed across the sky; thunder followed. Wind stirred the leaves. When Matt looked again, Eli was coming back from the kitchen. He sat down once more at the table. Matt gasped when Eli opened his hand—he was holding some of the lead discs that Matt used as fishing sinkers. Eli slipped the discs into the pouch. Then he removed several piles of coins from the table and placed them in the pouch, on top of the sinkers.

Matt immediately understood what Eli was doing. The lead discs in the bag would feel like gold. When Mr. Barrett opened the pouch, he would see only the coins on top. Eli had replaced enough gold in the pouch so that Mr. Barrett would be a long distance from the tavern before he discovered the theft. He might not even be sure where it had happened.

Eli scooped up the remaining piles of gold and filled his pockets. He was bending over, ready to insert the pouch back into Mr. Barrett's waistcoat, when lightning struck, followed instantly by a loud clap of thunder. Eli's head jerked up. He looked toward the window before Matt could duck out of sight. His eyes widened when he saw Matt, and his face twisted with rage. He raised his fist and shook it at Matt.

Matt remained rooted in place. Then fear took over. Eli

would kill him for spying! Matt dodged around to the rear of the tavern, but heard Eli open the back door. Matt turned and ran as fast as his lame leg allowed, through the pouring rain, toward the barn, hoping to find a place to hide there. Lightning flashed again, illuminating the yard like daylight.

"I see you, you filthy urchin!" Eli shouted. "Spying on me! Wait 'til I get my hands on you!"

Matt heard Eli's feet thudding across the wet ground behind him. He tried to run fast, but his lame leg hindered him. Now that Eli had seen him, there was no use heading for the barn. He would be trapped. Matt ran around the corner of the barn, heading blindly for the grove of trees that divided Eli's property from that of the neighbors.

Thunder crashed again, covering Matt's sounds as he fought his way through the undergrowth. His sleeve caught on a branch, but he yanked his arm loose and kept running until he stumbled over a log and fell. Eli's heavy footsteps disappeared around the side of the barn.

"You're going to pay for this if I have to hunt you all night!" Eli's voice echoed from behind the barn.

Matt shivered. The ground was sodden and cold. He rolled under a bush, gasping loudly for breath. He shivered again. He had to get away. Eli was still too close. Matt stood up and crept through the underbrush until he reached the far side of the grove. He stood for a second, looking out across the field. Although it was still raining hard, the storm was passing to the east. Eli's angry swearing rose above the sound of fading thunder.

Matt waited another second and then turned left, heading toward the river. The trees formed a barrier between him and the tavern yard. He skirted the edge of the field until he came to the road. Lightning illuminated the blackness so that Matt could see the boat shed across the road, silhouetted against the river and marsh.

Keeping low, Matt ran toward the shed as fast as he could, and hurried around to its far side. Rain splashed on the river, flattening the marsh grass along the banks. Matt heard Eli shouting from somewhere close to the tavern. Eli must have given up at the barn and doubled back, Matt reasoned. But there was still no safety here, he realized. Except for the shed, the ground was bare on this side of the road. He stood in the rain, his heart pounding, trying desperately to think where to hide next. Eli's voice sounded closer. Lightning flashed again, and in the brief second before darkness returned, Matt saw the skiff tied at the river's edge.

He darted from behind the shed and slipped and slid down the bank. Yanking the rope loose, Matt half fell into the boat and then scrambled to his feet. There wasn't a moment to lose. No time to fool with the oarlocks now. Grabbing the pole, he leaned forward and thrust it to the river bottom. The boat slowly edged away from the bank. Over the sound of the pouring rain, Matt heard the thud of Eli's boots crossing the road. Poling hard, he worked the skiff away from the tavern, keeping as low as he could. Darkness hid him, and the rain masked the sound of the boat cutting through the river.

Chapter Seven

"If there ever comes a time
when either my husband or I can
help you in any way,
you know where to find us."

Matt opened his eyes. He was lying on a small beach tucked against an overhanging bank. The sun was shining in a cleanly washed sky. What was he doing here? Last night's events came flooding back. Mr. Barrett, the storm, Eli. Eli! A prickle of fear ran through him. Matt bolted up and looked around. He was in a little offshoot from the river. The marsh stretched in front of him, empty. Only the calls of birds and the lapping of the water against the beach interrupted the silence.

He was safe—at least for a while. His clothes were wet, but the day was already warm, and they would dry. Matt stood up and stretched. He walked over to the skiff. Last night's rain had left an inch of water in the bottom. He pulled the skiff out of the stream, and digging his feet into the sand, slowly heaved it upward until it rested on its side. The water ran out. Matt dragged the boat back and floated it in the shallow water.

He climbed in, inserted the oarlocks and oars, and eased the boat into the river's channel. Instinctively, he headed downstream, away from the tavern. Blackbirds cackled at him from a thicket of trees, and a family of turtles, sunbathing on a log, plopped into the water as he drew near.

He had no idea where he was going or what he was going to do. Only one thing was certain: He was never going back to the tavern. Never! No matter what Mingo said, anything was better than living with Eli. And now that Eli had caught him spying, it would be dangerous to return. There was no telling what Eli might do when he got into one of his rages.

Matt kept a wary eye out for other boats. Eli was going to raise Cain at his absence. If someone spotted him on the river, the word would soon travel to Fast Landing and from there to the tavern.

Maybe Quinn would change his mind about letting him stay after Matt told him what had happened. So when he reached Indian Gut, Matt turned in and rowed down the waterway. But the dugout was missing from its hiding place, and Quinn's hut was empty. Something, maybe a raccoon, had knocked over the rain barrel so that there was no water. Nor were there any scraps of food in the hut, a sure sign that Quinn was gone for a long while. Matt made his way down the path, careful not to slip. He climbed into the skiff and cast off.

In the distance, vultures circled lazily over the marsh. The sun was hot and Matt's clothes were almost dry, but hunger pangs now gnawed at him. It must be noon, Matt thought. He hadn't eaten since early last evening, and not much then. Doggedly, he continued to row downstream. Rounding a bend, he spied a schooner heading upriver. He glanced around. There were no nearby waterways he could slip into and hide. There wasn't much time either; the ship was approaching fast. The crew might have already spotted him.

Matt saw there was only one chance. He headed toward the tall reeds lining the bank, shipped his oars, and grabbed the pole. Shoving hard, he worked the skiff as far as he could into the overgrown tangle of rushes, and lowered himself to the bottom of the boat. The reeds sprang back into place behind him. He peered over the edge of the skiff. The schooner was passing his hiding place.

Two men sauntered out on the foredeck. Matt held his breath. Neither looked in his direction. The ship passed out of sight around the next bend, leaving the skiff rocking gently in its wake. Matt sat up, shoved the reeds aside, and carefully maneuvered the skiff out into the channel again.

The hunger was a steady thing now, not just passing pangs. His stomach rumbled loudly. He felt light-headed from sun and lack of food. Drifting downriver, hoping to find something to eat, wasn't the answer. He would have to do something. Matt looked around the marsh. There weren't any berries, and, without a rod, he couldn't fish. His crab net was back at the tavern, so crabbing was out. What could he do, Matt wondered. The morning's optimism had vanished.

Sooner or later, somebody would be sure to see him if he stayed out on the river. Eli knew plenty of the men who hung around the wharf. They would be happy to do what a tavern keeper wanted in exchange for a bottle of liquor. And if Eli got word of his whereabouts, Matt was afraid he'd find a way to force him back to the tavern.

"Where you fixin' on goin'?" Mingo's words came floating back, unbidden. "At least here you got food in your gut and a roof over your head."

Matt was starving. Mingo had been right after all. Being hungry made him realize, for the first time, what he was up against. The sun beat down from a cloudless sky. Noon was long past. He tightened his grip on the oars and kept rowing. His head ached, and the horizon danced and wavered in the heat. He was thirsty, but there was nothing to drink. His lips were parched and he licked them, but it didn't help. Remembering the rainwater he'd emptied out of the boat made him thirstier still.

Finally, he slumped over the oars. Where could he go? Perversely, like thinking of the water he'd poured out of the boat, he remembered Mr. Hazard's store with its well-stocked larders. The boat bobbed up and down in the current as Matt pictured the hams hanging from the beams and the barrels filled with apples, pickles, and nuts. Then, suddenly, another voice floated into his consciousness: "I owe you a great debt for what you did for me today. If there ever comes a time when either my husband or I can help you in any way, you know where to find us."

It was his only chance. Matt nosed the skiff around and began rowing upstream. Thinking of Mrs. Campbell's promise renewed his strength. He pulled harder on the oars.

He didn't know how long he'd been rowing when he finally turned into Campbell's Creek. Edging the skiff alongside the dock, he threw a rope over a piling and pulled himself up onto the wooden planks. The place seemed empty. Only the vultures, more of them now, drifted in circles over the same spot in the marsh where he'd seen them earlier in the day. "Messengers of death," Pa used to call them.

Matt climbed the path leading uphill. Woods bordered the creek on his right. He stopped at the top to rest for a moment. The sun was shining in the western sky, while ahead of him, surrounded by trees, stood the brick house. It was a lot bigger up close than it looked from the river. For a moment, he was afraid. What if Mrs. Campbell didn't remember him? What if she'd forgotten her promise? He ran his tongue over his dry lips. At least they'd give him something to eat and drink. Squaring his shoulders, he limped across the lawn and around the side of the house.

Apple trees guarded the back door. Behind them was a neatly tended vegetable and flower garden surrounded by a white picket fence. Beyond the garden, he saw the farmyard with its barn, corncribs, and stable.

A gate opened into the vegetable garden, and, as he unlatched it, he saw a well, partially hidden by a tree. He hurried over and lowered the bucket, letting the rope slide through his fingers until he heard a splash. He pushed down on the windlass, pulled up the bucket half full, lifted it, and took long, deep swallows. Water ran down his throat, splashed over his chin and down his shirt front.

"Hey! What do you think you're doing?"

Matt jerked around. A boy, bigger than he, glared at him from the back doorstep.

"Where's Mrs. Campbell?" Matt asked, gripping the bucket tighter.

"What makes you think she'd want to see the likes of you?" the boy demanded.

"She told me to come see her if'n ev'r I needed help," Matt replied.

"Why would my mother want to help you?" the boy asked, eyeing Matt's bedraggled condition.

Matt's face flushed. It had been a mistake to come here,

he thought, but it was too late now. "'Cuz I helped her once't," he answered. He placed the bucket on the ground. His stomach hurt from drinking the water so fast.

The gate swung open behind him. Turning around, Matt saw Sam, the coachman. "You 'member me, Sam? From the day in town when the horse tried to bolt?"

Sam hesitated for a moment and then smiled. "Sure 'nough, I do! Lucky thing you wuz there. Otherwise, Mrs. Campbell, she would've bin hurt bad."

The Campbell boy looked puzzled. He turned and disappeared inside. Sam nodded at Matt and followed the boy into the house.

Matt sat down on the edge of the well. Thoughts raced through his mind. What was going to happen to him? He had half a mind to go back to the creek and take off in his boat, but he had to get something to eat first. He was dizzy from hunger.

Chapter Eight

Matt sat still. It was curious,
but Matt felt as though
his own will had left him.

The door opened. Matt looked up and saw Mrs.
Campbell descending the steps. She crossed the yard
and stopped in front of him. He looked at her silently.
Would she remember her promise?

"Hello, Matt," she said kindly.

"Kin I have somethin' to eat, ma'am?" He didn't mean
to blurt it out like that, but he couldn't help it.

"Of course, but what's happened to you?" she asked.
"You're a sight!"

Matt looked down at himself. Mud caked his feet and
legs. His trousers were torn and dirty. The shirtsleeve
he'd snagged on the branch while running away from Eli
was ripped.

"My son told me you were in trouble," she said.

He evaded her eyes and instead looked up at the big
brick house and at the lawns and pastures stretching down
to the water. Sheep and cattle grazed in the fading daylight.
Mrs. Campbell would never understand what life in a
tavern was like. He stared at the ground, not knowing where
to begin.

"Sam!" Matt heard her call. "Come here. I need you."
The door slammed and Sam appeared. "I want you to heat
some water and give this boy a real bath in the barn," she
instructed.

Matt half rose to his feet. "I guess I kin do my own
washin'," he said.

"No," Mrs. Campbell replied firmly. "I want to help
you, but I can't have you coming into the house until
you're clean."

Matt looked around frantically. Sam had already
disappeared. "Maria, bring out some apple pie," Mrs.
Campbell continued. Matt sat still. It was curious, but Matt
felt as though his own will had left him. A moment later, a
black woman appeared, carrying a plate with pie. Matt
reached for it hungrily. Holding the plate in one hand, he
picked up the slab of pie with the other and bit into it. The

crust was crisp and sugary, the apples soft with a tart sweetness. He wolfed it down.

Tom came out and crossed over to where Matt was sitting. He had burly shoulders and was half a head taller than Matt. He looked Matt up and down slowly, just the way a farmer looks over a horse or cow before deciding whether to buy it or not. Matt stared back defiantly.

"Don't dawdle now, Matt," Mrs. Campbell interrupted. "After you're clean, you can have a real meal. And, Tom," she said, turning toward her son, "go through your clothes, see what you can find that might fit Matt, and bring them down."

Matt looked at the older boy. There was no mistaking the resentment in Tom's hard blue eyes. Matt got up and slowly walked toward the barn, conscious of his limp and Tom's eyes upon him. The creek water glittered at the bottom of the slope. He would leave as soon as he ate dinner.

When Sam was finally satisfied that Matt was clean, he went back to the house and returned with an old shirt and pair of britches.

"I done had my supper, but Maria says fer you to come and get yours," he said.

Matt dressed quickly, crossed the farmyard and went through the garden. He again thought about leaving right then, but the smell of roasting mutton drifted through the kitchen door. He hesitated a moment, then opened the door and entered the kitchen.

A huge brick-backed fireplace dominated the room's far wall. In it, an iron kettle hung from a chimney hook, and a long-handled skillet rested near the coals. Chairs were drawn up around a table in the room's center. Different-sized baskets hung from the ceiling, and a tall wooden cabinet held pewter plates, wooden bowls, and stoneware jugs.

The kitchen was empty, but a door leading into another room was ajar. Voices were coming from that direction. Again, Matt paused, but the pie had whetted his appetite, and he was famished. He limped across the kitchen and entered the other room.

There, Mrs. Campbell and several girls sat at a large table. Maria was passing a bowl of vegetables. Tom had rolled up his sleeves and was carving the roast. He scowled at Matt as the room fell silent. In the candlelight, Matt had an impression of blue-and-white-checked curtains, a patterned rug on the floor, and faces staring at him.

Mrs. Campbell's voice broke the silence. "This is the family dining room, Matt. Maria has set a place for you in the kitchen," she said gently. "If my husband gets back in time this evening, he will want to meet you."

Matt felt the same way he did the day the boys made fun of him in the marsh. He wished he could shrink inside of himself and disappear. He turned and, without a word, retreated. He sat down at the kitchen table and waited while Maria brought him a heaping plate of food.

"Now, eat slow," she said. "Don't go makin' yourself sick. Cato, Quash, and Sam—they've already eaten theirs."

Matt didn't know who Cato and Quash were, and he didn't care. He picked up the fork and started shoveling food into his mouth. Maria came back as he was finishing. She lit the candles. Tree frogs shrilled loudly from the darkness outside. Matt yawned. Sleepiness weighed down upon him. It was too late to leave now, he realized. He'd have to wait until tomorrow.

Mrs. Campbell came into the kitchen. "Feeling better now that you've had a good dinner, Matt?" she asked.

He stared at her for a moment before nodding. She seemed genuinely concerned.

"The girls are excited about your being here," she said. Matt noticed that she didn't include Tom's name.

"You look exhausted," Mrs. Campbell continued. "I was hoping to have you meet the doctor tonight, but I'm afraid he might be late. He'll have things to talk to you about, but that will have to wait. I'll show you where you're to sleep."

She turned and opened a door in the paneled fireplace wall that hid a flight of narrow, steep steps. "Follow me," she said.

Matt was too tired to argue. He followed her up the steps, past a landing, and up another flight of steps into a small room, tucked under the eaves, which was furnished with a rope bed, a chest of drawers, and a chair.

"I hope you'll be comfortable here," she said, smiling at Matt before leaving the room.

Matt slowly undressed and numbly sank onto the bed. He hadn't slept in a real bed since before the sheriff made him leave the cabin after Pa died. Remembering that reminded him of Eli. It took little imagination to picture Eli's mood since he'd run away. Miserably, Matt rolled over and faced the wall, trying not to worry about what would happen to him, or where he would go, when he left Journey's End tomorrow. Other people had families, but he was all alone. It didn't seem fair.

A door banged, and somewhere he heard a man's voice. Then it was quiet again. He closed his eyes and tried to blot tomorrow from his mind. The wind picked up and the trees rustled outside his window.

A woman's voice floated up. ". . . go back there!"

"What happens if . . . ?" a man's muffled voice answered indistinctly.

Vaguely, Matt realized the voices carried through the fireplace from a room somewhere below. He closed his eyes again, too tired to care.

Chapter Nine

As Matt maneuvered the skiff
closer, a vulture raised its ugly,
bald head and eyed him balefully
from the far side of the dugout.

W hen Matt opened the door of his room the next morning, he spied another door across the landing. Opening it, he found an attic filled with old boxes and cast-off furniture. He closed the door and went downstairs. Nobody was in the kitchen, but men were talking in the dining room.

"I tell ye, Caleb, something's got to be done about the situation!" A fist banged on the table for emphasis.

"I agree, Thomas, I agree," another voice answered. "'Tis a sorry state of affairs when pirates feel free to sail up a river in broad daylight to plunder a town!"

Matt stood quietly and listened.

"And to sail under false colors!" A fist banged on the table again. "Thanks be to our good Lord that when the ship anchored for the night, a prisoner escaped and gave warning to the citizens of New Castle."

Matt leaned forward, listening raptly.

"Yes, that gave the residents time to arm themselves," the man named Caleb answered. "That, plus the fact that the tide was running out to sea and slowed the pirate ship's approach, saved the town."

"Ye should have seen the people of New Castle, when I was there on business last week, though. Nervous as old Nellies, they were. It'll be a long time before they forget what happened."

"Who can blame them?" Caleb said. "If the Quakers weren't so peace-abiding, we could give the pirates something to think about. They're regular blackguards!"

The door swung open, and Matt jerked around. A girl appeared, carrying a tray with tea cups.

"Hello," she said. "I'm Letty." She put the tray down. Matt looked at her. She was slim and short, probably about ten years old.

"Mama's upstairs with my sisters and Will. He's only six months," she said. "She asked me to tell you to wait down here, so she can talk to you later."

Matt looked into her blue eyes, trying to see if he was going to be asked to leave. Not that it really mattered, he thought. He was leaving, whether they knew it or not, as soon as he'd had something to eat.

Letty looked back at him calmly. Pale brown hair framed her oval face. "Do you want me to fix you some breakfast?" she asked.

"No," he said, straightening his shoulders and shifting his weight onto his good leg.

"There's plenty of food if you're hungry," she offered again.

"I can do fer myself," he replied gruffly, wishing she would leave him alone.

She waited for a moment and then, as if she'd read his mind, said, "Well, I best be getting back to help." He nodded. She hesitated, then turned and climbed the stairs.

Matt looked around the kitchen and saw the remains of a ham and some biscuits. He took a plate from the cabinet, cut some ham, and helped himself to the biscuits. Matt gobbled the food hurriedly as his glance roamed the room for food he could take with him. Since Quinn was away, he'd need enough to last a couple of days. The sound of chairs scraping the dining room floor interrupted his thoughts. The door opened. A stocky man, with graying brown hair, entered the kitchen. A younger man followed. They stopped at the sight of Matt.

"Ye're the boy my wife talked about," the older man said, giving Matt a warm smile. Then he pulled his watch out of his pocket and frowned.

"We're late and must go check the crops. I'm sorry, lad, to give ye such a short welcome to Journey's End, but we're glad to have ye with us. There're things I want to discuss with ye, but we'll have to talk later. Just wait here."

Matt looked at them. Everybody wanted to talk to him—but later.

The house was quiet after they left. Matt got up and

peered outside. No one was in sight. He went to the foot of the steps. From somewhere up above, he heard a soft murmur of voices. Moving quickly, he climbed onto a chair and lifted a large basket down from the ceiling. He found a clean piece of sacking and unfolded it. Scooping up the rest of the biscuits, he threw them into the cloth and added a loaf of bread from the back-oven. Next, he tore off a piece of the sacking and wrapped it around the remaining ham. What else? He looked around. An almost-full round of cheese sat on the ledge of the cabinet. He wrapped it in the sacking and added it to the basket.

He went to the steps again—Mrs. Campbell was talking to someone upstairs. Then, he removed an empty stoneware jug from the cabinet, and carried it and the food basket outdoors. Matt filled the jug at the well, left the garden, and hurried through the orchard. Far off on the right, he saw men cutting wheat. Their long, curved blades, swinging in unison, flashed in the morning sunlight. Drawing a deep breath, Matt left the cover of trees and started across the lawn. He turned left at the fence post, where masses of orange tiger lilies bloomed, and headed down to the creek. The tide was coming in, and his boat tugged at its mooring.

Nobody saw him. Out of sight from the main house, he quickened his pace. The basket was heavy and bumped against his leg. He walked out on the dock and looked down the creek toward the river. There were no boats in sight. He lowered the basket into the skiff, climbed in, and cast off. When he reached the mouth of the creek, he glanced up and down the river. Still no boats. Matt maneuvered into the channel and headed upstream toward Indian Gut.

Today was as different from yesterday as night was from day, Matt thought. Yesterday, he'd been starving and wet. Today, his stomach was full and he wore new clothes, even if they were hand-me-downs. And he was on his way to Quinn's with enough food to last a couple of days. The river sparkled in the sunlight. Every now and then, he turned in the boat and looked over his shoulder, but he was the only traveler on the river. Red-winged blackbirds clung to the tips of the tall grass and flashed across the marsh. The breeze was from the east, carrying the salty smell of the bay.

He'd covered a good distance when he saw, rising above the marsh grass around the next bend, the sails of a boat heading upstream. From the looks of her, she was the packet boat from Appoquinimink. Ahead on the right, its entrance half obscured by reeds, a narrow waterway led deeper into the marsh. He rowed toward it and turned in.

The waterway continued straight for a bit, then jogged left. Matt worked the skiff down its length and around the bend until he saw the sails sweep majestically upriver, billowing against the clear, blue sky.

He relaxed. Ahead of him, the waterway widened, beckoning him onward. He had nothing better to do. Why not, Matt thought, picking up the oars and following the stream. Here and there, the muddy bulges of muskrat houses rose from the marsh. The gut began to twist like the letter S. The rank smell of dead and dying vegetation was stronger here than out on the open river.

As Matt rounded the second loop, he saw an empty dugout pulled up against the bank. It was an odd place for someone to leave a boat and go out into the marsh. The odor was stronger now. He rowed nearer and stopped for a better look. Suddenly, he stiffened. There was no mistaking the high, curved bow of Quinn's dugout. What was he doing in these backwaters?

As Matt maneuvered the skiff closer, a vulture raised its ugly, bald head and eyed him balefully from the far side of the dugout. Then it squawked and rose cumbersomely into the air. Matt took his pole and pushed against the dugout's stern, working it horizontally toward the bank. It was then that he saw the vulture's prize.

A body, hidden by the dugout's prow, lay partially

submerged in the water. Matt stood up and poled closer. The body was lying face up, with its head resting on the muddy bank. When Matt leaned forward for a better look, Quinn's bloated face stared up at him blankly. From somewhere, an empty cry rang out across the marsh. It took a moment for Matt to recognize the sound as his own voice.

He half fell, half sat in the skiff. The boat rocked. The pole slid out of his hand, and he instinctively grabbed for it. Quinn, or what was left of him, bobbed up and down in the water. Matt remembered the vultures circling over the marsh a day ago. It must have been low tide. Now, the incoming tide had frightened them away, all but the one he'd just chased off. His stomach heaved. He leaned over the side of the skiff and vomited. He clung to the skiff's side as spasm after spasm wracked his body. It seemed to Matt as if all the contents of last night's dinner and this morning's breakfast spewed out of his mouth into the muddy creek water.

When the spasms were over, he straightened up and wiped his mouth with the back of his sleeve. Quinn's face looked back at him, his lips drawn into a contorted grimace. Now that the first terrible shock had passed, Matt noticed the small hole, rimmed with dried, darkened blood, staring at him like a third eye from Quinn's forehead. This was no accident, Matt realized. It was a bullet hole—Quinn had been shot!

Matt looked around at the empty landscape. He had to get help. He couldn't leave the body out here for the vultures to finish their gruesome feast. Who could help him? Mingo? No, Mingo meant Eli.

He crossed his arms over his knees and laid his head on them. What could he do? The sun beat down. After a few moments, he sat up. There was no getting away from it— he'd have to return to Journey's End. In spite of the fact that the Campbells would know he'd stolen the food, he'd have to do it! They weren't the kind of people who would let vultures pick the flesh off a dead man's bones. But first, he'd have to somehow protect Quinn's body. The vultures would return as soon as the tide ebbed. He looked around. There was nothing but waving marsh grass as far as he could see.

Matt threw one leg and then the other over the side of the skiff. He held on a moment and then slid into the water, his feet sinking into the thick, black ooze on the bottom. He shivered as the cold, murky water swirled around his thighs. He waded toward the dugout, grabbed the stern, and pulled it toward him. He jumped, almost losing his balance, as something brushed against him. It was Quinn's leg, the pants cloth stretched tightly over the swollen flesh.

Matt gripped the dugout tightly, fighting down another wave of nausea. When it passed, he eased the dugout next to Quinn's body. Bending over, he lifted the boat half out of the water, turned it, and lowered it over the Indian. The prow rested in the mulch, covering Quinn's head and part of his body. The tide was running out; the dugout would stay there, at least until the next high tide.

Matt waded back to the skiff and hauled himself aboard, dripping rivulets of muddy water over the bottom. He picked up the oars and began rowing quickly down the gut. The odor evaporated as he approached the river, making him feel better physically. Inside, though, he felt numb, blank, empty.

Who had shot Quinn and why? Matt pulled harder at the oars. Right now, he had to get back to Journey's End. There would be time for thinking later.

When he reached Campbell's Creek, Matt turned and looked backward over his shoulder. A lone vulture rode the air currents, circling lower and lower over the spot where Quinn lay.

Chapter Ten

All three looked up at the sound of
running feet outside. Cato burst through
the door, breathing hard. "Fire!
In the marsh! Best come see, sir!"

Matt trudged up the hill past a thicket of overgrown shrubs. "Thief!" Matt heard the word at the same time that someone tackled him from behind. He pitched forward, face down, onto the lawn.

"I've got you now!" A fist smashed into his back. He recognized Tom's voice and tried to get to his feet, but Tom straddled his back, grabbed his head, and slammed it into the ground. The impact stunned him for a second. Pain shot through his head. He groaned.

"I'll show you! Stealing our food, and after we'd taken care of you!"

Matt tried to roll over, but Tom hunched down tighter, pushing Matt's shoulders into the ground. "Let me up!" Matt gasped. A fist crashed into his back again. His stomach heaved.

"Tom! Stop that and get up!" Dr. Campbell's voice rang out sternly.

"He stole our food!" Tom shot back in a belligerent tone.

"Get up! I want to talk to him," his father ordered.

Tom reluctantly got to his feet and dusted off his trousers. Matt began to sit up, but another wave of nausea washed over him, and he started to retch. He lay on the grass wracked by dry heaves. When the spasms passed, he slowly sat up. His head ached and his back hurt where Tom had hit him.

Dr. Campbell studied him. "What's wrong with you, lad? Are you sick?" he asked.

Matt tried to answer but couldn't. He closed his eyes for a moment, only to be confronted by Quinn's face with its three eyes staring up at him.

"He's nothing but a low-down thief, Father!" Tom insisted.

"Let me take care of this, Tom. Now, boy, what's the matter with you?" Dr. Campbell asked again.

This time the words came out. "It's Quinn," Matt responded.

"Quinn? Who is he?"

"He's an Indian. Only he's dead," Matt said, fighting to remain calm. "I found him in the marsh—shot in the head." Tom and Dr. Campbell stared at him.

The doctor squatted next to Matt. "When did it happen?" he asked in a kinder tone.

"I'm not sure." Matt hesitated. "Yesterday, maybe." He rubbed his hand across his eyes. "I seen a lot of vultures flying over a place in the marsh. That's where I found his body. He's still there." He looked at Dr. Campbell. "I've got to git him away from there 'fore the vultures finish him! He's my friend!"

Dr. Campbell placed a hand on Matt's shoulder. "You did right, lad, in coming back to report this."

"How do we know he didn't do it?" Tom demanded.

Matt gasped and struggled to his feet.

"You stole our food! You could've shot the Indian!" Tom challenged.

Matt found his voice. "Quinn was my friend!" he shouted. "I'd never hurt him!"

"How do we know you're telling the truth?" Tom asked, glaring.

Matt turned toward the doctor, tears scalding his eyes. In horror, he dashed them away with the back of his arm.

"That's enough, Tom!" Dr. Campbell said. "Matt wouldn't have come back here if he'd shot the Indian!" He paused for a moment. "I think Sheriff Evans should be notified about this. A murderer's on the loose."

Both boys stared at him.

"I'll have to take a look at the body," he continued. "Tom, you saddle Gypsy and ride into town. Tell the sheriff to get out here as soon as possible."

"Yes, Father," Tom answered. Matt looked at the older boy. The sullenness was gone. He turned and ran toward the barn. Matt recoiled, sensing that Quinn's death was nothing but a lark to Tom, an adventure.

"Wait here," Dr. Campbell told Matt. "I'll be back in a

moment." He strode up the path. Matt rubbed his head, trying to organize his thoughts. The harder he tried, the more they spun in circles. Quinn, the vultures, Tom, the sheriff, Journey's End. He gave up. A moment later, a black horse galloped by with Tom hunched low in the saddle. They disappeared below the crest of the hill.

The doctor returned, his footsteps crunching on the gravel path. "I've got to go see a patient," he said to Matt. "I want you to stay here, but bring the food up from the boat before it spoils in this heat." He looked at Matt. "What made you take our food and run away, boy?"

"I don't know, sir," Matt mumbled, unable to figure how he could feel uncomfortable here in spite of the Campbells' kindness.

"Well, go get the food and give it to Maria. Have her clean you up. You're dirty, and Mrs. Campbell will never let you into the house like that."

Matt looked down at his muddy pants and feet. At least he wasn't as dirty as yesterday. And Dr. Campbell's promise to help with Quinn gave Matt a glimmer of hope.

"I'll git the food rightaways," Matt told Dr. Campbell, who was turning to leave. Matt took the basket around to the kitchen and silently handed it to Maria. She pursed her lips and slung it on the table.

"Go back outside and wait," she ordered. "I'll see that you git somethin' to eat."

Matt sat down under a tree and leaned against its trunk. His shoulder hurt where Tom had hit him. Maria brought him some cheese and bread and a cup of milk, but he found he wasn't hungry.

He ate only half the sandwich and leaned against the tree again, staring into the distance. It was hot, and he was grateful for the shade. The baby cried from an upstairs room. Once, he'd had a baby sister, but she'd died right after birth. And then his mother had died soon afterward, "from fever," Pa had explained.

Matt felt that he didn't fit in at Journey's End, and Tom's attitude made everything worse. He decided to stay through Quinn's burial, and then leave. He could always go back to Quinn's hut. Quinn has—had, he corrected himself—a barrel for collecting rainwater, Matt remembered. And somewhere, there were traps for catching animals. It would be lonely, but it was a place to stay. Matt closed his eyes.

The clip-clopping of a horse's hooves woke him. The trees cast long shadows across the lawn. He must have slept for quite a while. Shading his eyes with his hand, Matt saw Tom trotting up the drive. He closed his eyes again, pretending to be asleep, hoping Tom would leave him alone. No such luck. Tom rode toward him and dismounted. He had ridden hard. Dark sweat stains covered the horse's neck and flanks.

"Is that all you've got to do—sleep?" Tom asked in a scornful tone.

"Where's the sheriff?" Matt asked, sitting up straighter.

"Away—but they said he'd be back tomorrow or the next day. I left word for him to come here as soon as he got back." He moved closer to Matt. "Who was Quinn?" he asked.

"An Indian," Matt answered. He felt uncomfortable sitting on the ground while Tom stood over him.

"An Indian!" Tom exclaimed. "I thought they all migrated westward a couple of years ago. How come you knew him?"

Matt shrugged. "He was my friend," he said curtly, resenting the prying questions.

Tom came closer and knelt next to him. "What was it like finding the body? I mean, what did it look like?" he inquired, his dark eyes alive with curiosity.

Matt stood up abruptly. "Don't y'know what vultures do to dead things? How they pick and pick with their beaks 'til there's nothing left?"

Now Matt was standing and Tom was kneeling, looking

up at him. Matt's fist clenched and unclenched. He wanted to smash Tom's arrogant face. Instead, he turned on his heel and limped to the well to get water to wash up.

As he lugged the water buckets across to the barn, Matt caught sight of the men trudging up the hill from the field, scythes resting on their shoulders. He was scrubbing mud off his legs when Sam came into the barn, looking worried.

"Cato seen the ghost lights de other night," he said.

Matt stopped scrubbing and looked at him.

"Yes sir!" the black man continued. "He said dey was dancin' all over de river the night you come here."

"What are ghost lights?" Matt asked.

"Ain't you heard 'bout ghost lights? Why, dey come after something turrible's happened. Folks 'round here say dey is a dead person's soul."

A clanging bell interrupted their conversation. Sam gazed at Matt for a long moment and then said, "Hurry up so you don't miss supper."

When Matt left the barn, he was surprised to see that dusk was falling. Cato, Sam, and Quash looked up when he entered the kitchen and then went back to eating. Matt sat down silently and helped himself to meat and potatoes. He picked at his food halfheartedly. Every now and then, he caught someone looking at him.

They were still eating when the doctor came in, looking hot and dusty. "Well, I'm glad to see ye're looking a mite better than when I left you this morning," he said, spying Matt.

Matt watched him silently. He didn't seem angry about the stolen food anymore.

"When ye're finished eating, lad, I want to talk to ye," he said as he disappeared into the dining room.

"He wants to talk to you 'bout the murder," Cato said.

Matt didn't answer.

"Strange goin's-on out in the marsh these days," Quash remarked somberly.

Matt looked at the three expectant faces. He shoved his

chair back and stood up. He didn't want to talk about Quinn.

In the dining room, Tom was at the table with the doctor. A curly-haired young girl nestled in the doctor's lap. Candles flickered against the table's dark, polished surface.

"Now, run to Mama, Lucinda," Dr. Campbell said, giving the child a kiss and setting her on the floor.

"Sit down, Matt," Dr. Campbell continued, pushing his plate aside and wiping his mouth with a napkin. "I don't like this business," he said, looking from Tom to Matt. "It's a shame the sheriff couldn't come. I wanted to get this tended to today." He nodded in the direction of the parlor, where the *plink-plink* of a pianoforte could be heard. "I don't want to upset the whole family. The less they know about this trouble, the better."

"They already know somebody's been shot," Tom interrupted.

"Yes, but we don't have to worry them more than necessary. Now, Matt, what size boat can get into the creek where the body is?"

"A small one," Matt answered. "It's only a little backwater."

"Did ye see signs of anyone else having been there—tracks or anything?" Dr. Campbell asked.

Matt shook his head. He felt uncomfortable sitting in the formal room. Tom stared at him across the table's width.

"There's no telling when the sheriff will get here," Dr. Campbell said. "It's not decent leaving the body in the marsh. Besides, I should examine it. I'll get one of my men to help, and ye come with us tomorrow, Matt, to show us the spot. Though, Lord knows, I hate to take the time away from harvesting." He frowned and ran his fingers through his hair.

"Can I go?" Tom asked eagerly.

"This isn't yer business, Tom," Dr. Campbell stated. "Besides, I need ye to help with the harvest." Tom looked sullen.

All three looked up at the sound of running feet outside. Cato burst through the door, breathing hard. "Fire! In the marsh! Best come see, sir!"

"What's there to burn out there?" the doctor wondered aloud, rising to his feet and following Cato. Matt and Tom jumped up and went after them.

Cato led the way across the lawn. It was almost dark; the trees were black shadows silhouetted against the evening sky. Cato hesitated for a moment at the edge of the pine woods and then said, "Here's the path." They followed him, single file, into the inky blackness. The ground was carpeted with pine needles. Matt slipped and grabbed a branch to keep from falling. The rough, shaggy bark scraped his hands. He hurried, slithering and sliding, to catch up with the others. A few minutes later, the sky lightened again and Cato led them out of the woods onto level ground. The marsh stretched in front of them, dark and mysterious. In the distance, flames leapt upward, the pale gray smoke rising and blending with the deeper gray sky.

Matt scanned the horizon, trying to get his bearings while the others watched silently. Then Matt knew, knew without a shadow of a doubt, what fueled the leaping flames.

"It's Quinn's hut," he said slowly, turning toward the others.

Chapter Eleven

A breeze caught the sail and filled it.
The shallop hesitated and then
responded to the wind. . . . The
skiff trailed behind.

S am was already hoisting the shallop's sail when Matt went down to the dock the next morning. The tide was out. Sam gestured for Matt to get in. "Doctor says we wuz to take this boat and tow y'er skiff behind to use in gittin' down the gut," he said. "The shallop's too big for small streams."

Matt lowered himself carefully into the shallop. Dr. Campbell joined them a few minutes later. He handed Matt a tarp and a coil of rope. Then he gave his instrument bag and a musket to Sam before climbing in himself.

"Best to be prepared," he remarked, settling himself at the tiller. "All right, cast off!"

The boat eased away from the shore. A breeze caught the sail and filled it. The shallop hesitated and then responded to the wind, its prow slicing through the water as it headed for the river. The skiff trailed behind.

Matt made his way forward and sat down. He didn't feel like talking to anyone. All night, he'd tossed and turned, thinking about Quinn. One moment he'd see Quinn's bloated body floating in the water, only to have it replaced the next moment by the memory of the Indian's burning hut.

Who had killed Quinn, and why, Matt wondered. Had the same person set fire to Quinn's cabin? Matt had drifted off to sleep once, lapsing into a dream about a giant vulture with a razor-sharp beak bending over him, its dark eyes glittering. He awoke in a cold sweat and had been afraid to close his eyes again.

The wind was blowing steadily, and the boat heeled as it turned into the river. Looking at the overcast sky, Dr. Campbell said, "A nor'easter's brewing—mark my words! We'll be hard pressed to finish harvesting before it rains." His brow creased with worry. The wind gusted, sending the shallop flying through the water, the skiff straining behind it. They'd just navigated a large bend when Sam shouted, "Look yonder!"

Matt turned his head and froze. In the distance, a black

column of vultures spiraled upward over the marsh, marking the spot where Quinn lay.

Dr. Campbell's mouth tightened. "'Tis plain to see we have a difficult task," he muttered. "Matt, keep a sharp eye out so we don't sail past the channel!"

Matt nodded. He couldn't keep his eyes off the swirling cloud of vultures. Would anything be left of Quinn, he worried.

They continued to make good speed and before long approached the area where the vultures wheeled and darkened the sky. Matt leaned over the side of the boat, searching for the entrance to the channel, while Dr. Campbell adjusted the sails.

"Up ahead!" Matt shouted. Sam sprang to his feet and grabbed the boom, while the doctor lowered the sails. The boat rolled sharply and then steadied itself. Dr. Campbell tossed the anchor overboard.

Sam hauled on the rope, and when the skiff was next to the shallop, the doctor tossed the rope and tarp into it.

"Hold it close, Sam," he said as he climbed gingerly from the shallop into the small boat. "Now hand me my musket, the tarp, and my bag. Carefully!"

When he was settled, he said, "All right, Matt. Ye hold the skiff, so Sam can change boats."

"What about me?" Matt asked.

"Ye're not coming," Dr. Campbell said. "I need you to guard the shallop."

Matt looked at him. The shallop didn't need guarding! Then he looked toward the spot where he'd left Quinn. The air was thick with vultures, attracted by the smell of death. They circled lower and lower, their ugly red heads craning downward, searching for a landing place. Perhaps it would be better to stay in the boat after all. He'd help bury Quinn when they got back to Journey's End.

"All right," he said.

The doctor lifted the musket and, pointing it at the

vultures, squeezed the trigger. The shot echoed across the marsh. With raucous cries, the black mass of vultures exploded into the air. Sam began rowing down the channel. Matt watched as Dr. Campbell reloaded the musket and fired again. Another flock of vultures rose from the marsh, squawking angrily. Then the skiff disappeared around a loop. Matt settled down to wait. A dozen or so vultures still hovered over the spot. Another shot rang out, and, circling higher and higher, they too disappeared westward.

The shallop rocked gently in the river's swell. Matt looked at the low, scudding clouds. The only sound was the wind moaning across the marsh. A large crab, its eyes protruding on stalks, scuttled across the mud. Matt shuddered, thinking of Quinn lying on the muddy bank.

He didn't know how much time had passed before he saw the skiff coming back down the channel. As it got nearer, Matt saw Quinn's dugout trailing behind. Sam rowed the skiff alongside the shallop. Matt saw the grim expression on Dr. Campbell's face. Then he looked at the dugout. The tarp was wrapped and tied around something in the bottom. He didn't have to ask what it was.

He grabbed hold of the skiff to help the doctor climb back into the shallop. Sam remained in the skiff. Dr. Campbell knelt near the centerboard and pried open a section of decking. He reached down and started handing rocks to Matt. "These are ballast. Pass them to Sam," he said.

"Put them in the dugout's bow, Sam!" Dr. Campbell called. When he was satisfied there were enough, he motioned for Sam to pull the dugout next to the shallop.

Matt tried not to look too closely. He was grateful that the gusting wind was blowing the worst of the smell away. As Sam piled the rocks into the dugout's bow, it sank lower and lower into the water.

"All right," Dr. Campbell said. "Let's bow our heads and have a moment of silence."

"Here?" Matt cried, suddenly understanding what was

happening. "Is this where you're goin' to do it? You're not goin' to bury Quinn back at the farm?"

Dr. Campbell shook his head. "There's hardly anything left to bury," he answered. "I couldn't even perform an examination. And the smell, boy! It would be too much on the trip back. I'm sorry, but this is the best way."

The doctor lowered his head, and Sam did the same. Matt swallowed hard and looked at the bundle resting in the dugout. It seemed so little to him.

He lowered his head. It was the same as when Pa died—he couldn't think of a prayer. Dr. Campbell raised his head after a few moments. "All right, Sam," he said.

Sam leaned sideways out of the skiff and shoved hard on the dugout's prow until it ducked under the surface. As the muddy water swirled into the bow, the dugout slid deeper toward the bottom, its stern rising high in the air. Matt watched helplessly as, with a loud gurgle, it sank out of sight. For a few moments, a stream of bubbles floated to the surface. Then there was nothing, only the sound of the wind blowing over the marsh.

"Climb aboard, Sam," the doctor ordered. Matt looked at him resentfully. Quinn's death was as meaningless to him as one of the bubbles that floated up from the river's bottom.

When Sam was back in the shallop, Dr. Campbell set sail for Journey's End. Matt sat silently in the bow, staring ahead, not seeing the passing landmarks. He was all alone. Ma had died and the baby, too. Then Pa. And now Quinn was gone—down where the crabs and eels would finish him off. Mingo was the only person Matt had left. And Matt couldn't see or get to him because of Eli.

The boat lurched. Matt looked around and saw Dr. Campbell making his way toward the bow.

"Do ye know something about the Indian that ye haven't told me?" he asked, searching Matt's face.

"No, I bin thinking on it ever since I found him," Matt replied.

"Do ye know who his friends were, or, maybe I should say, enemies?"

"I never seen him wit nobody," Matt answered.

"Was he in trouble?"

"He didn't talk to me 'bout nothin' like that. Only 'bout huntin' and fishin' and the marsh," Matt said.

"Then ye have no idea who might have shot him?" the doctor asked. "Or why?"

"No, sir," Matt replied, looking Dr. Campbell straight in the eye.

"All right, boy," the doctor said, ruffling Matt's hair. "I thank ye for yer help in finding this godforsaken spot. Ye've had a rude shock. I'll leave ye be for a while." He turned and made his way back to the stern.

But in the back of his mind, Matt remembered Quinn, the last time he'd seen him, staring off into space, refusing to answer his questions about the strange boat.

Matt looked backward. The sky pressed down, casting a gray pallor over the river and marsh. The vultures were returning, wheeling lower and lower over the spot where Quinn had been shot.

Vultures! Matt thought bitterly. Where is the eagle to carry Quinn's soul up to the heavens?

Chapter Twelve

"Another pair of hands around the place would be welcome. I'm not asking ye to work out in the fields, but there's plenty to do around the barn and farmyard."

There was no dawdling around the table after dinner that evening. Rain, which had started soon after they'd finished storing the last of the wheat in the barn, lashed the windows. Everyone was exhausted, mercifully cutting short the number of questions about Quinn.

Matt had helped with the last of the harvesting after returning from Quinn's burial. Then, he'd fallen asleep on top of his bed, too tired to undress. Once during the night, he heard a whippoorwill's mournful cry, but he rolled over and went back to sleep. The next morning he awoke early and lay quietly, letting his mind wander. The rain started up again, drumming on the roof. He couldn't leave in this weather; besides, he had nowhere to go now that Quinn's hut had burned. He thought of Quinn, or what was left of him, lying on the river's bottom. What had he known that made someone kill him? Finally, Matt got up and descended to the kitchen.

"Matt's here!" Letty said as he walked in.

He awkwardly shifted his weight to his good leg. Tom glanced at him, pushed his chair back abruptly, and left the room. Puzzled, Letty watched him go. Then she turned to Matt.

"I have to help my sisters in the schoolroom," she said, excusing herself. Did Letty dislike him too, he wondered.

Matt remained at the table after eating, staring blankly at the rain. He weighed his situation. Only the skiff belonged to him; even the clothes on his back belonged to someone else. There was nothing to do and nowhere to go.

"Matt, Dr. Campbell and I want to talk to you in the parlor."

He looked up, startled. Mrs. Campbell had entered the kitchen. He got to his feet and followed her. They crossed the dining room, then the wide stairhall, and entered a large room furnished with chairs and tables. A mahogany secretary dominated one wall.

"Come in, lad, and have a seat," Dr. Campbell said,

putting down the book he was reading. Matt perched himself on the edge of the nearest chair. Mrs. Campbell sat down on a stiff-backed sofa.

"I'm glad yesterday is over," Dr. Campbell continued in a kindly tone. "That was nasty business. Best to put it behind ye as soon as ye can." He glanced through the window at the relentless rain. "I guess the weather has held the sheriff up." His expression became frustrated.

Matt said nothing. What good could the sheriff do now, he thought.

"Now that the harvest's in and things have calmed down, I've got some questions to ask ye," Dr. Campbell said.

"I've already told Dr. Campbell about your parents, the tavern, and what you did for me in town, Matt," Mrs. Campbell interrupted.

"Yes, my dear, ye did. And I'm grateful to ye, boy, for the assistance ye gave my wife. She promised to help if ever ye needed it, and so she has, and gladly too. But we've had no explanation of why ye are here." He looked at Matt expectantly.

Matt swallowed and looked down at the blue and red patterned rug. He didn't blame them for wondering. He rubbed his hands nervously on the arms of the chair. The material was cool and smooth to the touch.

"What happened to make ye come to Journey's End?" Dr. Campbell asked again.

If he told the truth, the part about Eli stealing the money, it would only cause more trouble. Besides, he doubted whether anybody would take a boy's word, an orphan's word, against that of a grown man. He stared out the window. Rain streamed down the glass.

"Answer me, Matt," the doctor ordered.

Matt shifted in his chair. The room was silent. A sudden gust of wind rattled the shutters. He cleared his throat.

"Eli owns the tavern," he started. "He was rough on me." He stopped, not knowing what to say next. The fire hissed in the fireplace. "He drank a lot—more and more these past months," he continued slowly. "He beat on me." His face tightened. "Seems like it was gittin' worse all the time."

Mrs. Campbell clasped her hands.

"All right," the doctor said in a gentle tone. "I can understand why ye ran away from the tavern." Then his voice became grim. "But I can't understand why ye stole our food and ran away from Journey's End."

Matt looked at the rain again. "I went to Quinn's first," he admitted. "But he weren't there. There weren't no food nor nothin' and I was awful hungry. I didn't know where's to go. Then I 'membered what Mrs. Campbell said—that she'd help." Then came the hard part. He swallowed again. "I knew Quinn'd be back sooner or later. I just needed some food to tide me over 'til he got back."

"That was stealing, lad!" Dr. Campbell said. "If ye'd asked, we'd have given ye some food."

Matt felt his face burning. He couldn't answer. He looked down at the floor again. What did a ham, some cheese, and biscuits mean to them, he thought bitterly.

"Ye planned to camp out in the marsh with the Indian?" the doctor asked. "Then what would ye have done?"

"I don't know," Matt answered truthfully.

Dr. Campbell leaned forward in his chair. "Are ye indentured to this man, Eli? Did ye sign any papers?"

"No, sir," Matt replied. "I got meals and a place to sleep after Pa died, in exchange fer helpin' out."

"Does he have any idea where ye are?"

Matt shook his head.

"The doctor and I have been talking," Mrs. Campbell interrupted. "You're welcome to stay here, Matt, if you'd like."

It wasn't what he'd expected, not after stealing the food and running away. He stared at her, not knowing how to respond.

"Yes, boy," the doctor said. "Between my medical

practice and this farm, I'm a busy man. Too busy. I rent out a lot of land to tenant farmers, but another pair of hands around the place would be welcome. I'm not asking ye to work out in the fields, but there's plenty to do around the barn and farmyard, particularly in the warm months when Cato and Quash have so much work. The vegetable garden always needs attention. Ye can probably give Maria a hand getting firewood and helping haul water from the well, too."

The doctor stood up. "I've got accounts to attend to, but I promise ye: Journey's End is a far sight better than a tavern! I'll have a word with Eli next time I'm in town. Even though ye're not indentured, I'm sure he'll not be happy to lose ye. I'll work things out," he concluded gruffly.

Matt didn't know what to say. He frowned, remembering Tom's hostility. Then he looked out the window at the pouring rain. He really didn't have much of a choice. For a moment, his mind flashed back to the last time he'd seen Quinn. The Indian was standing on the bank, watching the eagle's flight. If Quinn hadn't been murdered, it would've been so perfect. Living free on the marsh, hunting and fishing. He sighed. Well, Journey's End couldn't be worse than Eli's, he figured. He shifted in his chair and looked at the Campbells.

"I'll do my best," he said.

Chapter Thirteen

"You know what folks say—a
whippoorwill's a spirit
wailin' for all the things he's
left undone in his life."

The weather did not improve the following day. Interludes of brightening skies alternating with pouring rain forced everyone to remain indoors. Matt was in the kitchen when Tom came in from outside, shaking water off himself like a dog. He looked at Matt. Resentment hung in the air, as real as the clouds outside. Matt stood up and, without a word, limped across the room and left by the door Tom had just entered. He squished across the yard to the barn.

Cato and Quash were sitting on sawhorses, talking. "Yes, sir!" said Cato emphatically. "A whippoorwill's a spirit, not a bird. That's for certain! My mammy told me when I was a young'un. Look how nobody kin ketch one! Just when you think you're close, the sound gets further away, same as a spirit does."

"You're right," Quash replied. "I've heard a whippoorwill callin' the last couple of nights. It's that dead Indian's spirit. You know what folks say—a whippoorwill's a spirit wailin' for all the things he's left undone in his life."

"That true?" Matt asked, brushing the wet hair out of his eyes.

"Yes, sir!" Cato said. "You don't think that Indian knew somebody was goin' to shoot him, do you? The callin' is his spirit mournin' fer things he's got to do yet."

Matt considered the idea. "If'n you're right," he said, "Quinn's spirit is sad 'cause he can't fish nor hunt no more."

"It's more than huntin' or fishin' that Indian's grievin' for," Quash said soberly before standing up. He climbed the ladder to the loft; Cato followed. They began forking hay down to the barn floor. Matt stared after them, a puzzled look on his face. Could a whippoorwill really be someone's spirit? Did Cato and Quash know something about Quinn?

After lunch, Dr. Campbell looked out the dining room window and exclaimed, "If this weather keeps up, we'll never be able to start threshing!" He turned to Matt. "I might as well take a look at yer leg, lad."

Matt was caught off guard. "Can you fix it?" he asked.

"At yer age, to be truthful, probably not," the doctor conceded. "But I still want to have a look."

Matt followed the doctor down the hall and into his office. Ma had always wanted him to see a doctor, but they'd never had enough money.

"Have ye always been lame, or was it an accident?" the doctor asked.

"I was born like this," Matt mumbled.

"Get undressed," Dr. Campbell said gently.

Matt unbuttoned his britches and stepped out of them. The doctor probed his leg. He took Matt's foot and tried flexing the lower part of his leg, but it was stiff and wouldn't extend fully.

"It's a pity," he said. "The muscle tone's badly atrophied. There's nothing I can do. I'm sorry, lad. I wish I could help."

"Atrophied?" Matt didn't understand.

"Yes, atrophied, shriveled. There's no way to repair the damage."

Matt sat silently, absorbing the information.

"There's worse things in life than having one leg a bit shorter than another, my boy. I've known many a young sprout who didn't live to be yer age. Malaria, measles, accidents, and Lord knows what else claim many victims. Ye're in good shape except for yer leg." He cleared his throat. "Ye best get dressed."

Dr. Campbell was right. It could be worse, but that didn't make it any better. It was easy enough for the doctor to say it, but the doctor wasn't lame. He didn't have any idea what it was like to never being able to keep up with others and always have people stare at you. Silently, Matt pulled on his britches. He hesitated at the door.

Dr. Campbell looked up, a concerned expression creasing his brow. "What is it?"

"Nuthin', sir," Matt mumbled.

"Be thankful for yer health, Matt," the doctor advised kindly. "Learn to be thankful for what ye do have, and try not to fret about what ye don't have. That's one of life's big secrets," he said, dismissing Matt with a wave.

Matt limped down the hall. Someone started playing the pianoforte in the living room. As Matt approached the doorway, Letty called out, "Matt, come here!"

He didn't want to see anyone. He felt like crawling into bed and getting away from people, but it was too late— Letty had seen him. Matt stopped at the threshold.

"What did Papa want you for?" she asked.

"Nuthin'."

"Papa doesn't ask people into his office for nothing," she replied.

She was poised on the edge of the pianoforte bench. Had she heard anything? Then he remembered that the pianoforte had started playing just as he was leaving Dr. Campbell's office down the hall. She had overheard his conversation with her father! Matt's mouth tightened. Did she feel sorry for him?

Before he could accuse her of eavesdropping, she said, "I was helping Maria in the springhouse all morning, Matt, and when I got back, Mama told me you're staying! I'm glad. Come over here and I'll show you how to play a tune."

Matt felt his face turning red. "I don't know nuthin' 'bout music," he said.

"I'll teach you. There's nothing else to do in this nasty weather."

"I don't want to," he replied abruptly.

Her eyes widened. He hadn't meant it to sound the way it did. "Well, if you don't want to . . . ," she said, her voice trailing off. Her eyes searched the room, and Matt knew she was looking for a peace offering. "Do you know about the hidey-hole?" she asked.

"What's that?"

"It's a secret place to hide things," she told him.

"Grandfather had it built into this room. Mama stores our valuables in it."

Matt looked at Letty's wide eyes. He regretted his rudeness.

"Where is it?" he asked.

"See if you can find it," she answered.

Matt looked around, confused.

"I'll help you," she volunteered. "It's on this side of the room." She indicated the fireplace wall.

The wall was paneled across its entire width. Reeded pilasters framed each side of the fireplace, floor to ceiling. Matt limped over to the wall and studied it carefully. He couldn't see any sign of a hiding place.

"I'll show you," Letty said. "But don't tell anyone I did." When she stood up, her head barely reached Matt's shoulder.

She shoved a stool close to the fireplace and climbed on it. Running her hands across the surface, she called, "Look!"

To Matt's amazement, Letty had opened a cabinet in the paneling above the right side of the fireplace. The reeded pilaster seemed to be some kind of a frame.

"Now look," she called, fumbling inside the cabinet.

He watched as the chimneybreast over the fireplace swung open, revealing a large space.

"Come see," Letty said, nimbly hopping down from the stool. "There's a hinge you push down, inside the small cabinet, that opens the chimneybreast panel."

Matt crossed to the fireplace and looked up.

"You'll have to get on the stool to really see," she said. "Here, I'll help you."

"I don't need yer help," he said, embarrassed. Holding on to the mantle, he carefully climbed onto the stool, putting most of his weight on his good leg. He looked inside the hidey-hole. The space was much larger than he had thought. The cabinet on the right, although narrower, was deep, running back to the outside wall of the house. The large cabinet was equally deep.

"There's room to store everything important in the whole house!" she said. "And there's lots of fresh air, I guess from the chimney.

"See the hinge inside the right-hand cabinet?" Letty asked. Matt peered inside and saw the hinge. "If you press against it and shove down hard, it opens and closes the door to the chimneybreast. Isn't that clever?"

Matt shoved down hard on the hinge, and the door started to slowly swing shut.

"Once, my sister Prudence and I hid in the big cabinet to tease Tom," she said. "He couldn't believe we could fit in there."

"Kin see why," Matt answered, carefully stepping down.

A door opened down the hall.

"Quick! Papa!" Letty whispered, climbing onto the stool and closing the door to the cabinet on the right.

Dr. Campbell's footsteps echoed along the hallway, then began climbing the stairs.

"Don't ever tell anyone that I showed you the hidey-hole!" Letty said. "It's our secret." She put her fingers to her lips and smiled. Her eyes, large and expressive like her mother's, sparkled in her pale face.

Matt looked at her for a second. Her eyes had seen only the good side of life. "Don't worry. I won't," he assured her gruffly. Then he turned and limped toward the kitchen.

Chapter Fourteen

"Someone's comin'," Quash
remarked. A man was riding up
the drive. "It's the sheriff."

The constant rain was making everyone irritable. The sheriff hadn't come, nor had there been any word as to when he would. The rain gave Matt plenty of time to think about Quinn, but he was no closer to having any answers. Sitting in the kitchen, he went over and over his last visit to Quinn's place. His thoughts kept time with the steady rhythm of Maria kneading dough and Sam tapping his foot on the plank floor. Matt remembered Quinn, puffing on his pipe and refusing to answer questions about the strange ship. Maybe Quinn's death was related to the ship. But Matt couldn't imagine any connection. Quinn had always been moody: cheerful one moment, withdrawn and silent the next.

Matt watched Tom come down the back steps into the kitchen. When he saw Matt, Tom scowled and disappeared into the dining room.

"Master's son don't like you," Sam observed.

Matt shrugged. "I don't like him neither."

A little later, Letty appeared. "What are you doing, Matt?" she asked.

"Nuthin'," he muttered, embarrassed. "Waitin' on dinner, I guess," he added, to be polite.

"I came to get some wool so I can teach Prudence how to card," she said, rummaging through the large basket her mother kept near the spinning wheel.

"She's sure a help to her mother with those young'uns," Sam commented after she left.

"She's got real sense for a twelve-year-old," Maria added.

"Twelve?" Matt couldn't believe it. "She don't look that old," he said.

"Don't look twelve?" Maria asked. "Why, she'll turn thirteen afore the trees shed their leaves. I kin 'member the day she was born."

"She sure is small," Matt said.

"Slight, like her Ma," Maria replied. "Now, take Tom. He's fifteen, and near filled out like a man." She took a pinch of salt from the salt box hanging near the fireplace and sprinkled it over the swelling dough. "Yes, sir," she said. "She's small, but she's growin' fast."

The next day, the sun finally peeped through a hole in the clouds, brightening the sodden landscape. Water droplets sparkled like jewels on the leaves of trees and shrubs. The creek had risen, its muddy waters whirling only a hand's span below the dock. Matt pitched in to help rake the litter of leaves and downed branches from the lawn.

That afternoon, Matt and Quash were threshing oats behind the barn. As if to make up for all the rain, the weather had turned hot and steamy. Perspiration trickled down Matt's face as he flailed the stalks of oats against a screen and watched the chaff separate from the grain.

"Someone's comin'," Quash remarked. A man was riding up the drive. "It's the sheriff."

Both watched from the shelter of the barn as Sheriff Evans dismounted and strode up the brick path. He knocked on the door. A few moments later, Dr. Campbell admitted him.

"He's come 'bout the Indian," Quash said.

Matt stood still, but his mind was racing. The sheriff hadn't seen him. Dr. Campbell had promised to talk to Eli the next time he was in town and explain to Eli what had happened to Matt, but deep down Matt was afraid. Who was helping out at the tavern now? Mingo couldn't do all the outside work and the inside work, too. Dr. Campbell seemed confident that Eli would understand Matt's new situation, but Matt knew Dr. Campbell didn't know Eli. Even though he wasn't indentured to Eli, Matt knew that the tavern keeper was going to be angry when it came to reaching any understanding that involved losing Matt's services. What if Dr. Campbell couldn't make Eli understand? What if Eli insisted that Matt return to the tavern? Matt's stomach knotted at the thought of being forced to work for Eli again, particularly after he'd run away.

"I'll be back in a bit," Matt said to Quash. He skirted the corner of the barn, opened the gate into the garden, and crossed over to the back door. He stopped and listened at the top step. All was quiet. Maria must be upstairs with the older girls, he realized. The sheriff and Dr. Campbell were probably in the doctor's office.

Matt entered the kitchen. Dr. Campbell's voice was coming from the dining room. Matt tiptoed across the room and stood next to the door.

"It's outrageous, Joshua. No other word for it!" Dr. Campbell was angry. "To think of folks hereabouts who are willing to pay, PAY mind ye, to help form a local militia that would aid in protecting our coast, yet the Quakers refuse, on religious grounds, to contribute their share. And now, the Pennsylvania Assembly's backed them up!"

"I find it hard to believe, too," the sheriff replied.

"Ye know, Joshua, because we're a Crown Colony our counties have long supplied England with arms and materials during the wars with France and Spain. Now that we need aid, they won't help us. Our coast is completely undefended!"

Matt listened impatiently. What about Quinn, he wondered.

"I've just returned from a trip to Maryland. People everywhere are riled up about this," the sheriff said.

"And well they should be," Dr. Campbell retorted.

"Caleb, my friend, a man gets thirsty riding around in this heat. My drink needs refreshing."

Matt stiffened at the sound of scraping chairs. Footsteps started toward the kitchen. Matt looked around quickly. There wasn't time to get outside. He spied the door to the back stairs. A couple of steps, and he was there. He slipped inside and closed the door behind him. A second later, the men entered the kitchen. Matt sank down on the bottom step to listen.

"I could talk politics with you all day, Caleb. But the

message waiting for me when I got back from my trip was that you found a dead Indian in the marsh. Is that true?"

"Yes," Dr. Campbell answered and explained the sequence of events at Journey's End. "And there was no question he'd been shot," he concluded.

"Can you give me more details?" Sheriff Evans asked.

The doctor told of how Matt had found the body and returned for help.

"And you say the boy knew the Indian?"

Matt listened intently through the door.

"Said his name was Quinn," the doctor replied. "Seems as though they were friends."

"Quinn? I know of him," the sheriff said. "A real loner. He wouldn't have anything to do with most people. That Indian had a reputation for being difficult. The murder might have been for revenge."

"The boy didn't know much about him except his hunting and fishing habits," Dr. Campbell noted.

"There may be more to this than meets the eye," the sheriff said.

"What do ye mean?" asked Dr. Campbell.

"How well do you know the lad?"

Matt leaned forward to hear better.

"Not well, but I like him," the doctor said. "He came here a few days ago. He's a real ragamuffin, but a decent sort, nevertheless. My wife had promised to help him if he ever needed it. The boy saved her from serious injury when her horse spooked in town one day."

"What do you know of his background?"

"Only that he worked at Eli's waterfront tavern. Meals and lodging in exchange for helping out," Dr. Campbell answered.

"Do you know Eli, the tavern keeper?" Sheriff Evans asked.

"I stopped there once," replied Dr. Campbell. "An unpleasant type. Only good thing about him is that I was able to get what I wanted to drink. With the pirates around, most tavern keepers have trouble these days getting liquor."

"Seems to be a problem up and down the coast," the sheriff replied.

"The lad's told me some things about the man I didn't like," the doctor continued. "There's no question he abused the boy. Why do you want to know so much 'bout Matt and the tavern owner, Joshua?"

"I had a letter waiting when I returned," the sheriff said. "Written by a Mr. Barrett and postmarked from Baltimore. Barrett was mad as a hornet. States that he recently spent a night at the tavern and was robbed of a great deal of money there. He didn't actually discover the loss 'til he arrived in Baltimore. Apparently, whoever robbed him substituted lead sinkers in his money bag, but left enough gold coins on top so that he didn't discover the loss for quite a while. He's sure that the robbery occurred at the tavern. He and his partner are leaving for the West on a fur-buying trip. The partner secured a loan for him, but Barrett plans to stop here to see me about this matter on his way back north."

"How can he be sure the robbery took place at the tavern?" Dr. Campbell asked.

"He swears he didn't stop anywhere else."

"What about paying his tavern bill?" the doctor persisted. "Surely he did some business in Fast Landing, maybe bought some muskrat skins? Seems to me he would have discovered the theft before he got all the way to Baltimore."

Upstairs, a door opened. Footsteps echoed along the hallway. Matt shrank against the wall. What if somebody came down the back steps? He breathed a sigh of relief when the steps continued along the hall.

"I'm only telling you what he said in his letter," the sheriff was saying. "I went to the tavern and spoke to this Eli. Asked him if he remembered Mr. Barrett. At first he didn't, but when I gave him the date and a description, he owned as how he did recollect someone by that name. I told him Mr. Barrett discovered he was missing a lot of money when he got to Baltimore."

"What did he say to that?" the doctor asked.

"Said he didn't know anything about it. Then I pointed out that Barrett was sure the robbery occurred at the tavern."

"What was his answer?"

"He got all excited. Banged his fist on the counter and swore 'til he was red in the face. He said if Barrett was robbed, the boy did it."

Matt started and leaned closer to the door.

"Ye mean Matt, the boy we've got here?"

"That's the name he gave. Said the boy was always trouble. He told me that the same night Barrett spent at the tavern, the boy disappeared and hasn't been seen since. Said if there was a robbery, the boy did it, and that was why he ran away."

Matt felt his face turn red. How dare Eli blame him! Then, with an awful sinking feeling, he realized how running away had made him the perfect scapegoat.

"It seems hard to believe," Dr. Campbell said slowly. "The lad doesn't strike me as that type. Both my wife and I like him. He's had a rough life, I'll grant you—no manners and little education—but he's helped out willingly around here. I'm sorry to hear this, very sorry. It does sound suspicious, however. Personally, I lay the blame on your predecessor, Sheriff Boyd, for putting a young boy in a place like that!"

Silently, Matt agreed.

"You're right," the sheriff said, "but that was before my time. Any idea where the boy is now?"

"Threshing oats with one of my men."

"I want to talk with him."

"All right," Dr. Campbell replied.

Matt heard their footsteps until the kitchen door opened and closed. Where would they think to look when they couldn't find him at the barn, he wondered. Matt decided he could watch them better from the window in his room. Leaping to his feet, he hurried up the steps. The hall was empty. He climbed the stairs to the third floor as fast as he could and closed the door to his room.

Matt peered out the window and saw a carriage coming up the drive. It stopped in front of the house. Mrs. Campbell climbed down, holding the baby. Lucinda followed, and all three disappeared inside. Matt heard the schoolroom door fly open and the clatter of feet on the steps as Letty ran down to greet her mother.

Again, his mind was racing. Nobody would ever trust him now. How could he make anyone believe it was really Eli who'd stolen the gold? After all, he did run away from the tavern on the same night that Eli had robbed Mr. Barrett. Worse, he had stolen food from the Campbells after all their kindness to him. And being an orphan meant that he had no one—*no one*—to help with his defense. He'd be jailed— maybe even hanged! Waves of panic washed over him. He'd have to get away from Journey's End!

Out of the corner of his eye, Matt saw Tom and Cato returning from the direction of the woods. They stopped under his window. Then Dr. Campbell and Sheriff Evans appeared from the direction of the barn. Quash was with them.

"Have ye seen Matt?" Dr. Campbell asked.

"No. Why?" Tom asked.

"The sheriff wants to ask him some questions," his father replied. "There's no sign of him around the barn. Maybe he came back to the house. Quash, go check the dock and see if his skiff is still there. Tom, you go up and check his room, though I doubt he'd hide in the house."

Chapter Fifteen

Tom moved toward the attic.
Matt squeezed farther into the
recess until the bricks pressed
painfully into his back.

S teps sounded on the kitchen stairs. Matt thought quickly. There was no way he could get downstairs without running into Tom. He opened the door and went out into the hall. There was only one place to go, and that was the attic storage room. He limped into the room and quietly closed the door.

It was dark. The heat suffocated him. A little sliver of light filtered through a tiny window near the top of one wall, revealing cobwebs and the dusty surfaces of the family's cast-offs. A hodgepodge of old trunks, broken chairs, and wooden crates littered the floor. Tom's heavy tread started up the attic stairs. Matt carefully picked his way across the room, toward the large chimney jutting from the opposite wall. He felt across its uneven brick surface. Nothing.

Moving to the side, he found a shallow indentation between the backside and the wall, barely large enough to squeeze into. He slipped into the opening and pressed as far back as he could. The chimney overhang cut off the trickle of light from the window, casting him into deep shadow. A bat, disturbed from its resting place, launched itself across the room with a frantic fluttering of wings, setting Matt's heart racing. He stifled a yell.

The footsteps reached the top of the attic stairs, then entered his room. Matt waited. The heat was unbearable. He heard a heavy piece of furniture being moved. Tom was looking under the bed. Sweat ran down Matt's back.

The footsteps came out into the hall and halted. Matt listened, every nerve attuned to Tom's movements. Tom moved toward the attic. Matt squeezed farther into the recess until the bricks pressed painfully into his back. He sensed Tom standing in the doorway. Perspiration trickled down Matt's face, but he didn't dare wipe it away. He closed his eyes. Tom entered the storage room. Matt's heart hammered against the walls of his chest—surely, Tom could hear it. Matt held his breath. Tom started across the room. Suddenly, the silence was splintered by a loud crash. "Tarnation!" Tom's voice rang angrily through the small room. "What's this dratted thing?" Matt heard the sound of something wooden being kicked across the floor.

More bats, disturbed by the racket, exploded from the rafters and darted around the room. Tom swore again, then turned and hurried out of the room, slamming the door behind him. Matt listened to Tom running down the stairs, then stepped out of his hiding place, sank down on a leather trunk, and wiped his face. He raised his head and looked around. The bats, the only witnesses to his narrow escape, had disappeared, swallowed by the gloom. A wooden crate lay on its side where Tom had kicked it.

Matt slowly got to his feet. Tom was gone, but there was no guarantee that someone else wouldn't decide to have a look up here. On the other hand, if he stayed in the storage room, he would suffocate from the heat. He would have to wait in his room and sneak back in here if it became necessary. He silently limped across the room and opened the door. The chatter of children's voices rose from below. He leaned for a moment against the door frame, letting the cool air wash over him. How could he escape from a house full of people, he wondered.

As the afternoon wore on and sounds of the household's comings and goings drifted upstairs, Matt realized that escape would be impossible until everyone at Journey's End was in bed for the night. He sat on his bed, one ear tuned to the stairs and the other to noises from below his window. He heard the sheriff bid farewell to Dr. Campbell. "Thanks kindly for yer hospitality, Caleb. Don't forget to tell that lad, Matt, I'll be wanting to talk to him."

About the time that the sun was slowly sinking toward the horizon, Matt heard steps approach the attic stairs. Again he slipped quickly into the storage room and closed the door. As his eyes adjusted to the dim light, the steps started up the stairs. He carefully made his way toward his hiding place behind the chimney. Light footsteps crossed the hall and entered his bedroom.

"Matt? Are you there, Matt?" a voice called softly.

It was Letty! Matt caught his breath. For a moment, he had an overwhelming urge to go to her and explain every-thing—all about Eli, and living in the tavern, and how Eli had stolen the money. But something kept him rooted to his hiding place. After a few moments, the steps crossed the hall and descended the stairs.

Matt returned to his room and lay down. He closed his eyes. If only they would all go to bed! He could take the skiff and leave. He had to get as far away from Journey's End as he could. He had to go where nobody knew him. Where nobody had heard of Eli or the Campbell family. Where nobody could ever connect him with the missing gold.

He shifted restlessly. If only Pa were here, Matt wished. He could ask him what to do. But Pa was dead. Ma and Quinn too. He sighed and rolled over in bed and closed his eyes.

Matt awoke suddenly. The room was dark. He lay on the bed listening. Then he tiptoed to the window. Katydids shrilled in the darkness. Far up in the inky blackness, a tiny crescent of a new moon hung in the sky. It must be late, he thought. Matt remained at the window, listening and watching. The house was silent.

He crept across the hall and slowly felt his way down both flights of stairs to the kitchen. At the bottom, he stood still, letting his eyes adjust to the darkness. The smell of roast chicken, rich and moist, clung to the room, but he didn't dare try to find something to eat. Putting one foot in front of the other, he began to pick his way carefully across the darkened room.

"Halt!" Tom's voice shattered the silence. "I've got him, Father!" Tom shouted.

There wasn't time to think. Matt ducked, and bending

low, scurried toward the door. He was yanking it open when Tom grabbed him roughly from behind, pinning his arms behind his back. Matt wrestled desperately, trying to break away. A black shadow materialized in front of him.

"Let me handle this, Tom," said Dr. Campbell. At the same instant, Matt heard the click of a musket's safety catch and saw the gleam of the barrel. What difference did it make, Matt thought. Let the doctor shoot him! With a superhuman effort, Matt tried to wrench himself away from Tom's hold. Tom twisted his arms harder and, moving quickly, threw him off balance. Suddenly, Matt found himself sprawled on the floor.

"Get up!" the doctor ordered.

Matt sat up slowly, rubbing his head.

"It seems as though ye're in more trouble than ye let on when we talked, boy. Robbery!" Dr. Campbell said angrily.

Matt waited, trying to collect his thoughts. Maybe he could make another dash for the door.

"Father said to get up!" Tom ordered, reaching down and grabbing Matt's arm. "Stole someone's gold and then took our food!" Tom accused, hauling Matt to his feet.

"The sheriff came here today," Dr. Campbell interrupted. "Came about the dead Indian, but he told an ugly tale as well. About a robbery at the tavern. What do ye know about it?"

Matt turned toward him. "I didn't steal nuthin'! I swear! It was Eli! He done it. Not me! I watched through the window. The night of the storm. He got Mr. Barrett drunk and when he passed out, Eli stole the money from his waistcoat. I watched him count the gold pieces. I swear it!"

"Liar!" Tom shouted.

"I'm not a liar!" Matt shouted back, trying to break away from him. "I seen Eli do it! He went and got the lead discs I use for sinkers and put a passel of 'em in Mr. Barrett's money bag. Then he put some of the gold back on top and pocketed the rest." Anger and frustration flooded over Matt. He was innocent, but they'd never believe him.

No one would. No matter what he said or what he did, everyone would always think he was guilty. He wished he'd never been born.

"Your sinkers?" Dr. Campbell said, interrupting Matt's thoughts.

"My fishing sinkers. He filled most of the bag with 'em. With the gold on top, nobody could tell the whole bag weren't filled with gold."

Dr. Campbell let out a whistle.

"You're making it up!" said Tom.

"I'm not!" Matt lunged, trying to break away.

"Stop it!" Dr. Campbell ordered. "This is beginning to make sense. Go on."

"There was a big clap of thunder with lightnin' and Eli seen me at the window. He grabbed a knife and came after me. It was rainin' real hard, and I can't run fast with my bad leg. He was goin' to kill me. I know it!" Matt was almost sobbing with frustration. "I found my skiff and got away. I couldn't stay there no more."

"Why didn't ye tell my wife and me all this the afternoon we talked with ye and asked ye to stay here?"

"You wouldn't have believed me!" Matt said. "My word agin a grown man's. Besides, you already thought I was a thief 'cause I took some food when I went to Quinn's. But I didn't take the gold. Nary a piece of it. I swear it!"

"So, Eli stuffed the money bag with sinkers and then put gold on top, thinking Barrett would be long gone before he discovered that he'd been robbed?" Dr. Campbell asked. At that moment, Sheriff Evans words began to come back to him.

"That's what I reckon," Matt replied.

"There's no proof!" Tom said. "You could've put the sinkers in the bag!"

"If'n I were the one who took the gold, I'd be a fur piece from this place by now!" Matt shouted at Tom. "I'd never've come back here!"

"Tom, the sheriff told me that the reason Barrett never

discovered the robbery until he got to Baltimore was because the robber had stuffed the bag with fishing sinkers, but filled the top of the bag with gold. There's your proof," Dr. Campbell concluded. "Why did ye disappear today?" he asked Matt abruptly.

"'Cause I heard you and the sheriff talkin'," Matt admitted. "I heard him say Eli was tellin' everyone I run away that night 'cause I'd stole the gold. The sheriff said he had to talk to me. I was afraid, so I hid."

"I looked for you. Where did you go?" Tom demanded.

"The attic," Matt replied.

"I looked up there," Tom said.

"Not hard enough!" Matt shot back.

"Any rate, I knew you were around somewhere because your boat was still here," Tom said. "See, Father? I told you I'd catch him!"

"Yes, but I'm glad I happened to be working late in my office, so I could help ye," his father answered. Then he turned back to Matt. "I believe ye, lad," he said. "It would be hard to make all that up and, besides, what ye said fills in the missing pieces of what the sheriff told me this morning." He paused and rubbed his chin. "Barrett will be stopping back here on his way north. The sheriff and I will take him over to the tavern and confront Eli."

Someone believed him, Matt realized. For the first time, Matt felt a glimmer of hope. But Eli would deny everything. What were the chances that people would believe his word against that of a grown-up?

"Are ye prepared to stay at Journey's End 'til Barrett returns?" the doctor asked.

"Father!" Tom exclaimed. Dr. Campbell ignored him.

"Ye will have to stay around the farm," the doctor continued. "We don't want Eli to find out yer whereabouts."

Matt thought quickly. It was as good a chance as any. He'd just have to hope that Mr. Barrett would suspect Eli and not him. If he ran away now, everyone would think he was guilty for sure. It would mean he'd be running the rest of his life.

In the distance, a whippoorwill called, its mournful notes floating on the still night air. Could it be Quinn's spirit, like Cato said?

"I'll stay," Matt answered.

Chapter Sixteen

"It's true," insisted Prudence. "Maria says so. You dropped a knife. That means the next person to come here will be a man. You wait and see!"

Over the next few days, life at Journey's End returned to normal. Tom's resentment toward Matt was stronger than ever.

"Sneak!" Tom hissed whenever he found Matt alone. Once he jeered, "Hey, Gimpy!" Matt flinched, pretending to ignore the slur, but inside he seethed with anger. Since Tom was bigger and faster, there was little Matt could do except avoid him.

Letty's behavior was the opposite of Tom's. She went out of her way to be kind whenever she could, even though she was devoted to her brother, too.

"Tom's all right," she said once. "You've just got to give him a chance to get to know you, Matt."

Matt shrugged, not wishing to argue. In truth, Tom did seem to dote on Letty, but then, who wouldn't like Letty, he reflected. Matt appreciated the girl's kindness with a gratitude that would have amazed her had she known its extent.

As June merged into July, the farm work increased. Barley and rye had to be harvested, and the men spent long hours in the fields. Matt was spared harvesting because of his leg, but all sorts of odd jobs fell to him. He did what was needed without complaining. The harder he worked, the less time he had to worry about his situation and the robbery.

One day, he was in the smokehouse getting a side of bacon for Maria. Just as he lowered the leather cord that held the bacon suspended near the rafters, a shadow fell across the doorway.

"What do you think you're doing? Helping yourself to more of our food?" It was Tom.

Matt let go of the rope and whirled around.

"Water Rat!" Tom sneered.

"Where did you hear that?" Matt demanded.

"Oh, all the kids in town call you 'Water Rat,'" said Tom. He laughed and turned to leave.

Matt kicked a piece of firewood across the floor, grabbed the leather cord, and lowered the bacon. Even here, he couldn't escape the "Water Rat" taunts. And now Tom would be sure to tell Letty. Maybe she too would think he was strange. Matt squirmed at the thought. He tore the bacon off the hook and carried it across the yard to the kitchen.

One hot day followed another. The trumpet vine draping the fence burst into vivid orange blooms, and white caps of Queen Anne's lace dotted the meadows. The barley and rye were harvested, and now the men worked shoulder to shoulder cutting marsh grass for cattle fodder. Dr. Campbell and Tom penned and culled the sheep for market.

The morning following the penning, Matt watched Tom and his father riding down the drive, a flock of noisy, milling sheep trotting before them. It was close to noon when he heard a horse galloping up the drive. He leaned against his hoe and watched as the rider pounded on the front door.

"Why, Mr. Pratt! What can I do for you?" Mrs. Campbell exclaimed when she opened the door.

"Ma'am, I need the doctor."

"I'm afraid he's gone for the day," she replied.

"Do you know where, ma'am?" he asked. "The baby's started."

"He went into town with our son to sell some sheep, but then he had other business . . . I don't know where. I'm sorry."

The man slapped his hat against his leg. "I don't know what to do. It's our first child, and something's not right. Sarah needs help!"

Mrs. Campbell looked at him for a moment. "I'll come," she said. "I'm not a doctor, but I've helped at many a birthing and have had five of my own."

"I surely appreciate it, ma'am. More than I can say. How soon can you be there?"

"I'll need to find Sam and tell him to get the carriage ready. I'll come as soon as I can."

"Thank you kindly again," he said. "I'll be on my way now—I've got to get back!"

"Matt!" Mrs. Campbell called, spying him in the vegetable garden. "Find Sam and tell him to hitch the carriage. And go to the springhouse and tell Maria I need her."

A half hour later, Sam was waiting near the front door with the carriage. Mrs. Campbell came out, carrying the baby in one arm and holding Lucinda with her other hand. Letty and Prudence followed.

"Letty, I'm going to take Lucinda to the Carpenters' for the day. I'm taking Maria with me too. She's good at birthings. I'm leaving you in charge of Prudence. Stay close to the house. Your father and Tom should be back sometime this afternoon."

Mrs. Campbell climbed into the carriage and settled the children. A few minutes later, Maria hurried out the door and joined them.

"Matt," Mrs. Campbell called from the carriage, "keep an eye on the girls. Don't let them get into trouble."

"No, ma'am," he said, watching the carriage roll down the drive. Letty and Prudence stood beside him.

"It's almost lunchtime," Letty said. "Come inside, Prudence, and help me fix some food. And Matt, can you chop some wood? Maria said we were running low."

Matt nodded and went to find the ax. He was busy splitting firewood when Letty called, "Lunch is ready!"

Matt hesitated when he saw the kitchen table was set for three people. He sat down awkwardly.

"All I could find was bread and butter and some apple pie," said Letty. "But that will do."

As he reached for his plate, Matt's arm brushed against the silverware, and the knife clattered to the floor.

"That means a man will be the next person to come into the house," proclaimed Prudence.

"Why?" Matt asked.

"Oh, that's what people around here say," explained Letty. "They believe if someone drops a knife, a man will be the next person to cross the threshold. If a fork is dropped, it'll be a woman. A spoon means it'll be a child."

"It don't make sense," said Matt.

"It's true," insisted Prudence. "Maria says so. You dropped a knife. That means the next person to come here will be a man. You wait and see!"

Matt ate as quickly as he could, and started gathering leftovers to take down to Cato and Quash.

"I've had all I want," Prudence announced, sliding out of her chair. "I'm going to play outside."

Matt crossed over to the fireplace and was bending over to open the bake-oven door when a crash came from the front part of the house. Next, he heard running footsteps.

"Who's that?" asked Letty, turning quickly.

Before Matt could answer, Quash burst into the kitchen. His eyes were wide and staring. Beads of sweat dotted his brow.

"Pirates!" he hollered. "Pirates!" He bent forward trying to catch his breath.

Matt and Letty stared at him.

"Lord have mercy!" Quash moaned. "They'll slit our throats!"

Letty screamed and clapped a hand over her mouth.

"Where are they?" demanded Matt.

"Comin' up to the dock," Quash answered. "I seen them on my way to the barn."

"Did they see you?" Matt asked.

"I don't know," replied Quash, grabbing the back of a chair and breathing hard.

Matt looked out the kitchen window. He glanced at Letty. Her hand was still clamped over her mouth. The woods bordering the lower meadow blocked the view to the dock.

"I'll go see," he said and hurried through the door into the dining room. He skirted the table and ran into the hall. Quash had left the front door open. Matt looked out and caught his breath. A large sloop with a long bowsprit and a single, tall mast was approaching the dock. It was the boat he'd been wondering about since April. Now it was coming to him! Above the billowing mainsail fluttered a small black flag. The mystery was solved. He slammed the door shut and slid the bolt.

"What did you see?" asked Letty, who had followed him into the hall.

"Quash is right," he answered. "Pirates!"

She stared at him for a second, then darted into the living room and looked out a front window.

"They're tying up," she said in a shrill voice.

Matt looked over her shoulder. A man was leaping from the sloop's foredeck onto the dock.

"They'll get Cato!" blurted Quash, who had followed them into the front part of the house.

"Prudence!" screamed Letty. She whirled around and raced from the room.

Matt watched helplessly. He felt he was in a nightmare in which something was chasing him but his legs wouldn't move. Only this time, it was real. He wasn't going to wake up and find everything all right.

Quash blundered across the room and began closing and locking the windows.

"That won't keep them out!" Matt said. His glance swept over the room and rested on the mantelpiece. The hidey-hole! He crossed to the fireplace.

"Bring a stool," he ordered.

Quash dragged the stool over. "What you goin' to do?" he asked.

Matt didn't answer. He climbed up and ran his hands over the chimneybreast. They both jumped as the kitchen door slammed.

"They're here! They've come for us!" Quash cried.

A child wailed. Footsteps hurried toward them. Matt felt a surge of relief.

"It's the girls," he said and went back to searching the chimney for the mechanism that unlocked the cabinets.

Letty appeared, holding on to Prudence, who was crying.

"The hidey-hole?" Letty exclaimed. Letting go of her sister, she rushed across the room.

Just then, Matt's fingers found the concealed spring, and he pressed down. The door of the right cupboard swung open. Leaning closer, he reached his arm inside and fumbled for a moment.

"Want me to help?" Letty offered.

"I can do it!" Matt said. The paneling above the fireplace began to spring open. The pirates were grouping at the bottom of the hill. Prudence was wailing on the other side of the room.

"Come here, Prudence!" Matt called to the frightened child.

Prudence cried louder.

Matt hurried across the room and grabbed her arm. "Stop that sniveling!" he ordered roughly, giving her a shake. "You and Letty will be safe in the hidey-hole. But you got to keep quiet. Understand?"

"I'm scared," she whimpered, choking back a sob.

"Matt's right, Prudence," Letty said. "Nobody knows the hidey-hole's there. I'll be with you. But if you cry, they'll find us for sure. Do you think you can keep quiet?"

Prudence gulped and nodded.

"Come over here, then," Letty said.

Prudence hesitated, but then ran to her sister. Quash and Matt dragged a large chair to the fireplace.

"Letty, you go first. Then you can help Prudence," Matt instructed.

For a moment, Matt thought that Prudence was going to start crying again, but she bit her lip and stayed quiet.

"Can you help me, Matt?" Letty asked. She was standing on the arm of the chair. With Matt's help, she clambered onto the back of the chair and hoisted herself into the cupboard. Once inside, she wriggled around so that she was facing out.

"Hurry up, Pru!" she called to her sister.

The young girl looked terrified, but Matt helped her scramble onto the chair. Letty reached down, grabbed her hands, and pulled Prudence headfirst into the cupboard. There was a scuffling as she adjusted herself next to her sister.

"All right?" Matt asked.

"I guess so," Letty said, but her face was pale, and she looked scared.

"I'm going to close the doors now," Matt told her.

"Aren't you going to hide in the other cupboard?" Letty asked.

"Too small," Matt said. He closed the door to the small cupboard, then shut the hidey-hole door firmly and climbed down. There was more scrambling as the girls positioned themselves.

Matt and Quash shoved the chair back into place.

"What are you going to do?" Letty asked, her voice muffled by the cupboard door.

"I'll find somethin' else," Matt answered. "Just be quiet."

Looking out the window again, Matt saw the pirates climbing the hill toward the house.

"Run, Quash!" he said. "Hide in the cornfield!"

Quash hesitated. "Are you comin'?"

"In a minute," Matt replied, knowing full well that he could never reach the cornfield with his bad leg before the pirates saw him.

Quash bolted from the room.

"Run, Matt! Hurry!" cried Letty.

"Hush up!" he ordered, moving toward the hall.

The door banged shut behind Quash. Matt hurried to the

kitchen. As he bolted the door, he caught a glimpse of Quash racing toward the cornfield. The pirates had reached the first clump of trees on the lawn. Matt turned to find a hiding place for himself.

Suddenly, a long, drawn-out scream split the air. Matt's blood ran cold. He swiveled around and looked out the window. Two pirates held Quash, while a third pointed a musket at him.

"Don't shoot!" Quash begged. "Don't shoot!"

The rest of the pirates gathered around and laughed.

"Matt, Matt, what's happened?" It was Letty calling from her hiding place. Doesn't the girl have any sense? He started toward the parlor, but then turned back. The pirates were dragging Quash across the lawn toward the path leading to the dock.

"No! No!" Quash shouted, struggling to free himself. As Matt watched helplessly, a pirate jammed a musket into Quash's back. Quash stopped struggling. The rest of the pirates then turned and headed for the house. Quash was being marched toward the ship; his captor held a gun to his back.

"Matt!" Letty called in a terrified voice.

He swore under his breath and hurried back to the parlor. "They're almost here!" he said. "Keep quiet! No matter what happens, keep quiet!"

A loud banging began on the kitchen door, followed by the sound of window glass tinkling onto the floor. A louder crash was followed by shouting, signaling that the pirates had broken through. There was no time to get upstairs, not with his bad leg. Matt turned and ran into the study. The doctor's big desk, solid across the front, stood on the far side of the room facing the door. Matt hurried around it, scrambled underneath, and curled up as tightly as he could.

Chapter Seventeen

A tall man stood in the doorway. . . .
A pair of pistols was jammed
through his wide leather belt. Gold
earrings dangled from his ears.

Matt huddled under the desk, listening to the heavy tread of feet reverberating through the first floor. Someone ran up to the attic and then down again. "Nobody's here!"

"But the door was locked from the inside!" a voice answered.

Matt heard someone come down the hall and turn into the study.

"Hey! Lookee here—a medicine cabinet! We've found a doctor's office!"

More footsteps hurried into the study. Someone yanked open the medicine-cabinet door. Matt shrank as far back under the desk as he could.

"But where's the doc?" a voice asked.

"Right here!" another voice answered boisterously. To Matt's horror, someone sat down in Dr. Campbell's chair and pulled it up to the desk. Matt felt his heart thudding against his ribs. Loud laughter erupted from the others. Matt scarcely dared to breathe.

"What's this?" the pirate said as his foot nudged Matt under the desk. Matt closed his eyes. He was finished! The pirate grabbed his leg and started pulling. Matt clawed at the carpet, but it didn't help. He found himself looking up at a circle of dirty, bearded men.

"Well, I'll be!" the pirate exclaimed. "Stand up!"

Matt stared at them, too afraid to move. The pirates crowded closer. All were armed with long, sharp knives or pistols.

"Get up, I said!" the pirate commanded, kicking Matt's side.

Matt winced and scrambled to his feet.

"Where're the others?" the pirate demanded.

"They're gone," Matt replied, his voice wavering.

"The truth!" the pirate ordered. "Where's the rest of the family?" he demanded again. The man shook him so hard that Matt's head snapped back and forth.

He stared into the fierce, dark eyes and felt his legs tremble. "They're not here," he said.

"Where are they?"

"Tom and his Pa—they drove the sheep into town. Mrs. Campbell—she and Maria went to help at a birthin'."

"Be ye a Campbell?"

"I'm Matt," he replied, trying to still the tremors in his legs.

"You're not one of the family?"

Matt shook his head. Would they carry him off just like Quash? Maybe Quash was already dead. His knees began knocking together at the thought.

"When will they be back?"

"I don't know," Matt answered.

"I asked a question!" the pirate said in a harsh tone. "WHEN will they be back?" He slammed Matt against the wall.

Matt's head jerked forward sharply. He looked at the circle of faces. "I don't know," he whispered.

"We caught a slave outside," another pirate said. "Be there more?"

Matt thought of Cato. He hoped that he was deep into the woods by now. "Two more," he said. "But one went with the doctor . . . and the other, he drove Mrs. Campbell in the carriage."

"Are you indentured?" one of them demanded.

Matt nodded. It was easier than explaining.

"We're wasting time, Buck!" someone in the back of the room shouted. "Let's see what we can find in the house!"

The pirate released Matt, who stumbled, grabbing a chair to keep from falling.

"Be the good doctor a surgeon?" someone yelled.

Matt looked across the room. A pirate was brandishing the surgical knives Dr. Campbell kept in the medicine cabinet. The room fell silent. Matt nodded. Was he imagining things, he wondered, or did they look pleased?

"All right, men," said the pirate who had grabbed Matt. "There's fine pickings for us here. Get to work!" He left the room. The rest followed. The one who had found Matt pulled him along.

"Wait 'til Captain hears we've found a gimpy servant lad!"

Matt's heart lurched. So they were going to take him prisoner!

The pirates swarmed into the parlor, dragging Matt with them. He tried not to look at the chimneybreast.

"Aha!" one of the men shouted, seizing a silver snuff box from a table. The others began snatching objects that caught their fancy. A pirate picked up a piece of porcelain and smashed it against the wall.

For a second, Matt thought he'd heard a whimper, but the pirates were making so much noise he wasn't sure.

"The Devil's book!" one called scornfully, holding up the Bible for everyone to see before hurling it into the fireplace.

They all turned at the sound of approaching steps. A tall man stood in the doorway, dressed in baggy dark pants that were tucked into leather boots. His gray vest was buttoned over a white shirt, and the sleeves were rolled up. A pair of pistols was jammed through his wide leather belt. Gold earrings dangled from his ears.

"Captain, nobody's here but for one gimpy lad!"

The captain eyed Matt silently. Matt saw that a scar ran down one side of the captain's face from his temple to his jawline. Behind him stood four more men. A babble of voices interrupted, as the pirates explained the whereabouts of the missing family. Matt leaned against a chair to steady his quivering legs. If only Letty and Prudence would continue to keep quiet!

"You say the doctor's a surgeon?" the captain inquired, surveying Matt with interest.

Matt nodded, not trusting his voice to a response.

"All right, men. Do your task," the captain said as he headed for the kitchen. The rest of the band followed, lugging their booty.

Matt hung back, desperately hoping for an opportunity to whisper something to Letty. A pirate grabbed his shirt collar and pulled him along. Four or five pirates, including the one holding on to Matt, headed upstairs. When they reached the second floor, they began ransacking the bedrooms. Matt stood with his back pressed against the wall of the Campbells' room. He watched as the pirates pulled the coverlet off the bed and tossed Dr. Campbell's two suits into it. They yanked open the drawers of the chest, adding the contents to the coverlet. Another began rolling up the featherbed. Mrs. Campbell's silver-handled brush and comb and silver shoe buckles were tossed into the heap. Everything of any value was stripped from the room. Matt pressed harder against the wall, half dazed with horror.

One of the men put on the doctor's wig and capered about the room while the others roared with laughter. From downstairs came the sound of china being smashed and furniture overturned. Shouts and raucous laughter echoed from the kitchen. What must Letty and Prudence be thinking? If only Prudence didn't start crying!

"Are you finished up there?" It was the captain's voice.

"Aye, we're done," a pirate replied.

Matt watched as they tied the corners of the coverlet together. One of them slung it over his shoulder.

The kitchen was a shambles. Broken china crunched underfoot as they crossed the floor.

"A toast to His Majesty!" bellowed a short, swarthy man, taking a swig from one of the Campbells' casks and raising his cup in the air. Loud laughter and thumping on the table greeted the remark.

Matt saw a tablecloth piled high with candlesticks, knives, forks, and pewter platters. Baskets overflowed with flour, sugar, salt, and tea.

"All right, men, time to move on before someone spots us," the captain said. He put down his cup of rum and stood up.

One of the men grabbed the cloth, knotted the ends, and hoisted it over his shoulder. Others grabbed the baskets of foodstuffs. Matt huddled in the corner, praying they'd forget him. He held his breath as they began trooping out the door.

"What about the gimpy boy?" someone called out.

"Bring him along," the captain decided.

Matt's heart sank. *I'm going to be taken prisoner! Like Quash!*

"Come on," the pirate said. "Captain wants you."

Matt remained motionless, his mind spinning with half-formed escape plans.

"I said come!" the pirate snarled. Grabbing his knife, he sprang toward Matt and pressed the sharp blade against his chest. Matt felt the knife prick his skin. There was no escape. He followed the others outside.

Pirates were running in and out of the smokehouse, stripping it of meats and casks containing Dr. Campbell's rum and whiskey. Others were filling jugs at the well. Several men appeared from the barn, hauling a cart they'd piled full of spades, lanterns, rope, and other farm items.

The pirate guarding Matt gave him a shove and nodded toward the barn. Matt followed him across the lawn. The new calf, born just three months ago, bleated in terror in a far corner of the barnyard. Chickens cackled and ran about in circles. One of the men found a large fishing net, tossed it over them, and drew it closed. Then he started toward the boat, dragging the net full of squawking chickens.

"Give a hand here!" a pirate snapped to Matt. "Captain wants the calf."

Matt watched helplessly as the man cornered the frightened animal, grabbed its head, and slit its throat. The calf let out an anguished squeal, crumpling to the ground.

Matt felt sick. He leaned over the fence and closed his eyes.

"What's wrong with you?" taunted the captain. "A little blood make you sick?"

Matt looked at him wordlessly.

"I'll cure you of that!" the captain assured him with an unpleasant grin. "Take the calf down to the boat!"

Matt climbed between the rails and limped over to where the calf lay on the ground. Its eyes were blank. Blood spurted from its throat, staining the sandy soil.

Matt swallowed hard and picked up its hind legs. He began dragging the calf across the lawn toward the path leading to the dock. He turned his head for a last look at the house. No sign of the girls. The calf was heavy, and Matt stumbled. All around him pirates were toting their booty toward the dock. The moored sloop strained against the tide.

The captain stood on the foredeck watching. There was no sign of Quash.

"Swing the calf over here," ordered the captain, gesturing toward the sloop's deck.

Matt swallowed again, gripping the calf tighter. He swung hard, but the calf was an awkward burden, and one of its legs slipped from his grasp. Matt clung to the other leg for a moment, and then, losing his balance, let go. The calf splashed into the creek and sank from view.

The captain scowled. "That boy's more trouble than he's worth!" he said. "We don't need a cripple aboard ship! Leave him behind!"

Matt stared in disbelief.

"Set sail!" the captain shouted. "Hurry up!"

The men cast off the lines, and the sloop slowly drew away from the dock.

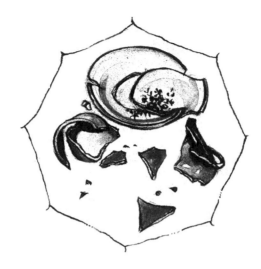

Chapter Eighteen

The flames flickered in the
evening breeze, reflecting
the damage. . . . Bits of china lay
scattered about the hearth.

Matt clung to a piling and watched the ship set sail for the river. He'd escaped! And all because he'd lost his balance and let go of the calf. For the first time in his life, his lameness had served him well.

The sloop heeled slightly as its sails filled with wind. The captain stood at the bow, his legs braced against the ship's roll as he looked back toward Matt. He cupped his hands around his mouth and shouted, "Tell the doctor we'll be back for him soon!" The words carried across the water and hung in the air.

A shock ran through Matt. Back? They were coming back for Dr. Campbell? He spun around and headed up the hill as fast as he could. He hurried through the house and into the parlor. Whimpering sounds were coming from above the fireplace.

"It's me, Letty," he called.

"Oh, Matt," she pleaded, "get us out of here!"

He pushed a chair over, climbed up, and pressed the concealed spring. The doors swung open. Prudence was crying, and Letty looked like she might start at any moment. When he helped them down, Letty flung her arms around his neck and exclaimed, "You saved our lives!"

Matt went rigid with embarrassment. After a second, she stood back. Her face was flushed. Prudence collapsed in a chair and cried harder.

"All we could hear was men shouting and things breaking, Matt. What happened?" Letty asked.

Matt described the pirates' rampage. ". . . and when I lost holt of the calf and it sank in the crick, the cap'n said I'd be more trouble than I was worth, so he let me go!"

Letty smiled and clapped her hands. Then her face darkened. "We'll have to check the house and see what else they did," she said, starting out of the room.

"Don't leave me!" Prudence wailed, jumping up and running after them.

Matt watched the grim expression on Letty's face as

they went from room to room. When they got to her parents' bedroom, she sank into a chair. "They've taken all Mama's pretty things. Broke things, too. They even took the feather-bed!" Her eyes filled with tears.

Matt wanted to console her. "They took a lot, but they didn't git us!" he said. "Though they got Quash," he added slowly.

"Quash! Oh, no!" Letty exclaimed. "I shall pray every night for his safe return," she said, taking a deep breath. She stood up slowly. "I guess we should start cleaning, Pru."

The three had almost finished sweeping the bedroom when Letty suddenly looked up. "What's that noise?"

Matt and Prudence stopped sweeping and listened. Then Matt heard it, too. Someone was creeping around downstairs! Matt put his finger to his lips and looked at the girls. He grabbed a poker from the fireplace and tiptoed to the head of the stairs. Footsteps entered the downstairs hall, then paused. Matt gripped the poker harder. His heart was racing; fear that the pirates had returned clutched at his stomach. Then Cato appeared at the bottom of the steps.

"The good Lord have mercy! They didn't git you!" he exclaimed at the sight of Matt. "What 'bout the others?" Briefly, Matt described what had happened.

"If only Quash hadn't gone up to the barn!" Cato said, visibly upset. "As soon as I seen that ship sailin' up the crick, I hightailed it for the woods!" He looked around. "They sure tore up this place."

"They took most of the food, too," Matt said. "Look around and see if'n you can find anythin' to eat."

Cato left. When he returned he had a basket filled with eggs. "They took most of the chickens, but I found these."

It was almost supper time when Tom and Dr. Campbell returned. Prudence flung herself into her father's arms as soon as he dismounted.

"What's wrong, Poppet?" he asked, smoothing her curls.

"Pirates, Papa! Pirates!" she sobbed.

"Pirates?!" he exclaimed. "Where're the others?"

"Everybody's safe," Letty said quickly. "Sam drove Mama and Maria to the Pratts' to help with a birthing. She took Will and left Lucinda at the Carpenters'. But Quash! They got him!"

Tom followed his father inside. He swatted the edge of the kitchen table with his riding crop. "They'll pay for this!"

Dr. Campbell hugged the girls. "How did ye escape?" he asked.

"Matt saved us," Prudence told him. "He put us in the hidey-hole over the fireplace and told us to be quiet."

Dr. Campbell stared at Matt for a long moment. "Ye have my wife's and my everlasting gratitude for the deeds ye've done today, lad," he said, giving Matt's shoulder a squeeze. His voice sounded strange, Matt thought, not at all like his normal, firm manner of speech. The doctor cleared his throat awkwardly. Tom looked at Matt, a funny expression on his face. Then he and his father made a quick survey of the house and outbuildings.

"They took everything!" Tom said.

"It could be worse," his father answered. "We're safe. The cattle and horses are all right, and we just sold the sheep. We can easily get more chickens. And, with time, we'll be able to take care of the damage in the house." His face grew somber. "But it's Quash I worry about. I fear for his life."

"I'll go get Sheriff Evans!" Tom declared.

"No, Tom, he can't do anything tonight. I'll go first thing tomorrow morning," the doctor said.

They were eating the eggs that Letty had boiled for supper when the carriage rolled up the drive. Dr. Campbell went out to meet it, cautioning the others to remain inside. When he returned, he had his arm around his wife's shoulders. She began crying at the sight of Letty and Prudence.

"Come, come," the doctor soothed her. "We should be thankful our lives were spared."

"I am thankful, Caleb," she replied. "And you, dear boy," she said, turning to Matt, "first you saved me, and now my daughters!"

Matt felt his face turning red. He looked down at his plate.

"We must thank the Lord for sparing our family, Caleb," she said, taking the baby from Maria. "I want everyone to go into the parlor so we can have a short prayer of thanksgiving."

Matt knelt near the fireplace and looked around the parlor. The others, including Maria, Sam, and Cato, knelt in a semicircle, while Dr. Campbell read from the Bible, which Matt had retrieved from the fireplace. Letty had found some candles. The flames flickered in the evening breeze, reflecting the damage. A table had a broken leg, furniture was overturned, and the sofa had been slashed in several places by a sword. Bits of china lay scattered about the hearth.

"Oh, Heavenly Father," Dr. Campbell intoned.

Matt bowed his head but couldn't concentrate. Instead, he remembered the sloop as it sailed down the creek. The captain's words—"We'll be back!"—echoed in his ears.

Chapter Nineteen

"I bought two new muskets in town this morning," the doctor continued. "And I bought a pair of pistols, too. I'm going to teach ye how to shoot."

E arly the next morning, Dr. Campbell took Matt and Tom aside and told them to stay close to the house until he returned from town. After he left, Tom turned to Matt and asked, "What was it like when the pirates were here? Were you scared?"

"Yes," Matt admitted curtly. "And you'd 'ave bin too!" He went back inside to help with the cleaning.

When the doctor returned later in the morning, he was wearing a new pair of pistols strapped around his waist.

"Sheriff Evans has gone to see the Marvels at Sherburn. The pirates also raided their property," he reported. "They tied everybody up and ransacked the place. Took three slaves captive, too! Everybody in town is talking about it. Seems they stopped there on the way downriver, after leaving here." He turned to Tom. "Saddle up and ride over to Sherburn. Tell the sheriff what happened here yesterday. Ask him to come to Journey's End as soon as he can. And, Matt, I need ye to help me with something in the barn."

"I wanted to talk to you away from the others, Matt," the doctor said when they reached the barn. "My business takes me away from the place a lot. After what happened yesterday, ye and Tom will always have to be here when I'm gone. Understand?" he said, looking directly into Matt's eyes.

Matt nodded.

"I bought two new muskets in town this morning," the doctor continued. "And I bought a pair of pistols, too. I'm going to teach ye how to shoot, Matt. Tom can already shoot as well as most men I know."

Step by step, Dr. Campbell showed Matt how to load and prime a flintlock. It was a complicated procedure. The doctor patiently reviewed it again and again, showing Matt how to pour the powder into the pan of the lock, how to hold the musket properly, and how to aim.

"I doubt I could do it all in time, if'n I had to," Matt said.

"Practice will give ye the hang of it," Dr. Campbell said.

"And don't forget—the other man has to go through the same procedure, too."

Matt squinted down the barrel. Then he put the gun down and looked at the doctor. "The cap'n said they was comin' back to git you," he said. "Why would he say that?"

The doctor looked startled. A frown creased his forehead. He stood still and looked seaward, rubbing his chin. Then he turned to Matt. "Pirates are always on the lookout for surgeons," he said. "Surgeons to care for their injured, and carpenters to build things. I'm sure he meant it when he said they'd be back." He rubbed his chin again, looking worried.

Matt looked down in dismay. It was all his fault! He was the one who had told the pirates the doctor was a surgeon. Now they'd be back. How could he have been so dumb? And after all Dr. Campbell had done for him!

"Did they say anything else?" Dr. Campbell asked.

"No, sir," said Matt, shaking his head. "But I've seen their boat before."

"Where?" Dr. Campbell asked, surprised.

Matt recounted the April day when the sloop had silently passed him in Herring Creek. "I've bin huntin' for it ever since," he added.

The doctor was quiet for a moment. "Look here," he said, "ye know yer way around the marsh better than anyone else I know. I think I'll give ye time to fish or crab now and then, and at the same time ye can do some scouting about the waterways. Let me know if ye see anything suspicious. Would ye be willing to do that?"

Matt nodded.

"Ye wouldn't be scared?"

"I'd be keerful," Matt said slowly. He looked out across the marsh and added softly, "Quinn must've found out 'bout the pirates. That's why they had to kill him."

Chapter Twenty

"I've got a hankering for a crab supper," Dr. Campbell said two weeks later, giving Matt a meaningful look.

The next morning, Matt was cleaning the mess in the barn when a shadow fell across the entrance. He looked up and saw Tom blocking the doorway.

"Better come up to the house," Tom said. "The sheriff will be here soon."

Matt hesitated.

"What's wrong?" Tom asked. "Are you scared?"

Matt remained silent. Deep down, he was afraid. What if the sheriff didn't believe him and arrested him for the robbery at Eli's tavern? The thought haunted him. He knew he shouldn't be so afraid. After all, Dr. Campbell seemed to believe him, but would that be enough? Eli was so crafty he could easily convince others that Matt had stolen the money.

"He'll only want to talk to you about the pirates," Tom said, as if reading his mind.

Matt looked at him. He seemed sincere.

"Sheriff hasn't come yet," Matt said, glancing down the drive. "I'll stay here." Tom shrugged and returned to the house. Matt resumed sweeping, every now and again stopping to look down the drive. At the sound of hoofbeats, he dropped the broom, slipped out of the barn, and hurried across the meadow. Once in the shelter of the woods, he turned and looked back at the house. The sheriff was dismounting near the front door.

Matt settled down at the base of a large oak to wait. A squirrel scrambled up the tree and chattered at him from the safety of a branch. From his vantage point, Matt could see the house. After what seemed like a long while, the sheriff reappeared and rode away. When he was safely out of sight, Matt returned to the barn.

He was filling water buckets when Dr. Campbell found him. "Where were ye?" he demanded.

Matt lowered the bucket and said, "I was afeared to see the sheriff."

"He wanted information about yesterday's raid."

"What if he asked 'bout the robbery?"

"I told him what ye've told me about the robbery, Matt," Dr. Campbell stated.

"Maybe he don't believe it."

"I know it looks bad, lad, real bad, but it's my experience that the truth will prevail," Dr. Campbell said. "Luckily, I could give him a pretty good account of what happened from everything ye and Letty told us yesterday. He couldn't stay long, at any rate. Said the whole area is in an uproar over the raids."

The day after the sheriff's visit, Dr. Campbell took the two boys aside and reminded them they had to stay around the house whenever he was away. "Ye two must always be here to protect the family," he said. "And keep the muskets handy."

"Yes, sir!" said Tom. It was easy to see that the prospect excited him.

That evening, Mrs. Campbell came into the kitchen. "Matt, would you like to eat with us in the dining room?" she asked.

Matt's head jerked up in surprise. At the same instant, he again felt the shame that had washed over him the first night when he stood in the dining room and had been told to eat in the kitchen.

"Thank you kindly, ma'am," he said after a pause, "but out here's what I'm used to."

The following days were filled with tallying what was missing and getting the house back in order. Whenever someone complained about the damage or stolen food and goods, Mrs. Campbell said with quiet determination, "We must give thanks that we are all together. And God have mercy on poor Quash, wherever he is now."

Several times, Sam drove into Fast Landing to buy goods or necessities. With Quash gone, Matt had to help Tom and Cato in the fields. More important, there was a change in Tom's attitude. Although he wasn't actually friendly to

Matt, the "Gimpy" and "Water Rat" taunts had stopped. Tom also no longer avoided Matt's presence.

Whenever he found time during these days, Matt went down to the lower meadow, nailed a scrap of red cloth to a tree trunk for a target, and practiced loading and priming the musket. He found the musket heavy and awkward to handle. Most of his shots missed completely.

"I've got a hankering for a crab supper," Dr. Campbell said two weeks later, giving Matt a meaningful look. "I'm staying home to catch up in my office. Why don't ye go crabbing?"

The day was hot, but the air was cooler out on the river. Puffy white clouds floated lazily overhead. Sunlight glinted on the water, becoming a thousand pinpricks of light whenever a breeze ruffled the surface.

Matt rowed steadily. His goal was Herring Creek. If he was to explore it and also bring home enough crabs for supper, he couldn't waste time. The river stretched ahead, bordered by a thin necklace of white beach, behind which the great marsh lay, golden-green, until it merged with the horizon.

Matt rested for a moment under the leaning pine tree just inside the creek entrance, then started rowing again. He passed the spot where he had caught the shad in April. The channel narrowed, but not as much as he remembered Quinn saying it did. There were no signs of pirates or their sloop. Everything was the same.

The only difference was that the gaunt, white tree trunk, blasted by a long-ago lightning bolt, no longer marked the distant hummock. A storm must have finally toppled it, Matt thought. It had helped him get his bearings the last time he was back this way, and he was sorry to see it gone.

When Matt started home, he had almost a bushel of crabs scrabbling around in a large basket. Dr. Campbell met him at the dock. "Any sign of pirates?" the doctor asked as he helped Matt unload the skiff.

Matt shook his head. "Nary a sign of anythin'," he replied.

Everyone ate steamed crabs for supper, dipping the sweet flesh into melted butter. Matt was helping Maria clean up in the kitchen when someone rode up the drive.

Mrs. Campbell came hurrying in and asked Maria to bring some wine and biscuits into the parlor. "Mr. Marvel from Sherburn is here," she said, turning to Matt. "The doctor wants you to join us."

Dr. Campbell introduced Matt to Mr. Marvel and said, "Tell him what happened when the pirates came here, Matt."

"They did much the same kind of damage at Sherburn, and took three of my slaves," Mr. Marvel said when Matt finished. He frowned and added, "I don't think my wife will ever get over the events of that day." He turned to Mrs. Campbell. "What concerns me is that this kind of thing can keep on happening. Nobody's safe!"

"But what can we do?" she asked. "The government pays no attention to us."

"We've got to fortify our coast!" said Dr. Campbell, thumping the table for emphasis. "It makes my blood boil when I think of the Pennsylvania Assembly refusing to approve defense money for our protection."

There was silence for a moment.

"We must write a letter to the governor in Philadelphia," said Mr. Marvel, rising to his feet and pacing around the room, "giving a full account of our losses and demanding protection!"

"An excellent idea!" agreed Dr. Campbell. "We'll point out how everyone along the coast lives in fear. We should insist they send a warship."

"Agreed!" replied Mr. Marvel. "Young Tom, fetch me some paper, ink, and a pen."

After the letter was drafted, Mr. Marvel read it aloud. "That should do it," he said. "And if it doesn't, I wager the Assembly will find it has a revolt on its hands the next time it tries to collect taxes from citizens living in coastal areas of our Lower Counties."

"I wish I'd been here when the pirates attacked," Tom said suddenly. "I'd have shown them a thing or two!"

"If you had any idea how evil those blackguards are, you would never make such a foolish statement!" Mr. Marvel said sternly. He took off his glasses and looked at Tom for a moment before continuing. "When Sheriff Evans came to Sherburn after the raid, he told me a grisly tale of a pirate captain who captured a Spanish ship. The captain had the Spanish crew bound up, and then sewn into the main-sail. He then ordered his men to toss the whole bundle—with the crew inside—overboard. They all drowned! That should give you an idea of what kind of devils we're dealing with!"

Tom, along with everyone else in the room, sat silently, shock clearly registered on their faces.

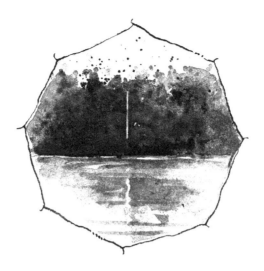

Chapter
Twenty-one

Then he looked again. It *couldn't* be!
There was the old pine, its white trunk
clearly silhouetted against the green
backdrop of the hummock.

July turned into August. Heat lay over the region like a warm, wet blanket. Horses and cattle sought shade under trees while their tails switched away flies. Thunderstorms rolled eastward across the land, dropping their rain. During several nights, when heat made sleeping difficult, Matt heard a whippoorwill's cries drifting mournfully through the darkness. They brought back memories of Quinn.

Under the surface of daily life at Journey's End lay the constant fear of another pirate attack. Dr. Campbell stayed home whenever he had the chance, having Matt take the skiff and go fishing. It was a good cover for exploring. Although Matt searched as many of the waterways as he could, he found no signs of pirate activity. But the fish he brought home helped to make up for the food the pirates had taken; extra fish were soon strung in the smokehouse.

One day, Matt rowed his skiff into Indian Gut to visit Quinn's old place. Weeds had overgrown the vegetable patch, and only charred remains were left of his hut. Matt stood on the rise and looked over the marsh. Quinn had known the whereabouts of the pirates' hideout. That's why he was killed, Matt figured. If only Quinn could send some kind of message to help him find their hideout! But all was quiet. Nothing stirred in the marsh.

Whenever he had the chance, Matt continued his target practice. One hot afternoon, after missing round after round, he jammed the musket butt into the ground in disgust. "Hey! Wait a minute! Never treat a gun like that!" He turned and saw Tom crossing the meadow.

"Here, let me show you." Tom took the musket and put it up to his shoulder. "You don't just hold it. You cradle it against your shoulder. See? Take a deep breath before you squeeze the trigger; it steadies the gun. Like this." He pulled the trigger. The red cloth fluttered as the bullet struck it. "See? It's easy," he said, returning the musket to Matt.

Matt stared at him. Tom wasn't boasting. He was trying to help. Matt took the musket and nestled it into his shoulder. He squinted down the barrel, held his breath, and squeezed the trigger. There was a puff of smoke, followed by a dull thud as the bullet hit the tree.

"Not bad," Tom encouraged him. "Try again."

Matt primed and loaded the musket while Tom watched and advised. By the end of the afternoon, Matt had nicked the cloth twice and made a direct hit once. The sun was beginning to set, sending red streaks across the gray, feathered sky.

"We'd best be getting back to the house," Tom said.

The boys started across the meadow, Tom slowing his stride so that Matt could keep up with him. Matt glanced at the older boy. What had gotten into him? Ever since the pirate raid, it was as if the old Tom with the hard eyes and cold manner had disappeared. Matt plucked a long piece of meadow grass and chewed it as he walked along, reflecting on the changes in his life during the past few months.

Several evenings later, Mr. Marvel paid another visit. "I bear good tidings," he said after dismounting. Matt took his horse, while the family gathered around. "I've had word from the governor in Philadelphia," he announced. "He's sympathetic to our situation and agrees the coastal areas need help. He promises to send a warship as soon as possible."

"Thank God!" said Dr. Campbell.

"Yes, thank the Lord!" echoed Mrs. Campbell, smiling.

Matt felt a prickle of excitement. A warship was really going to come! But a week went by with no sign of the warship. Then another week passed. Dr. Campbell became increasingly irritable, lashing out more than once at anyone slow to respond to orders.

Matt felt guilty. He knew the doctor was worried that the pirates would return. It didn't matter that Dr. Campbell had told him it wasn't his fault; Matt knew full well that it was. In the back of his mind he saw the pirate brandishing the knives and asking, "Is the good doctor a surgeon?"

And just as clearly, he remembered nodding his head—"Yes." Matt would have given anything not to have let the pirates know that Dr. Campbell was a surgeon. But they had already found the surgical knives. Besides, he hadn't known that pirates needed surgeons. He sighed.

The only positive thing was that he now worried more about the pirates' coming back than about Eli's accusing him of the robbery. One worry had replaced another.

"That damned Assembly!" Dr. Campbell swore one evening. "Always promising and not delivering, while we sit here helpless!" He paced about the room. Matt looked at him. He noticed there were dark shadows under the doctor's eyes and that he'd lost weight. It was clear to Matt that Dr. Campbell was really upset.

Matt went outside. The moon sailed high in the sky. Tomorrow would be a nice day, and Dr. Campbell had said that he'd be home in the afternoon. Matt decided he'd take the skiff out again. If only I can find where the pirates anchored their sloop, he thought, it would make it easier when the warship came. If it ever does come!

It was low tide when Matt set out the next afternoon. The sun was warm on his back as he headed downriver toward the bay. Little pools of water left by the high tide pocked the beaches. Shore birds darted about the river's edge, pecking at debris left by the receding tide. Matt had already explored the web of creeks and waterways near Journey's End. He figured that he might as well return to Herring Creek, where he'd first seen the pirate sloop.

When he reached the creek, Matt shipped his oars and rested for a moment, then resumed rowing. Tree branches hung over the water's edge, their lowest leaves dusky gray-green, marking the high-tide level. Dark, slimy roots of trees and shrubs, exposed by low tide, snaked across the oozing mud that edged the creek bank.

Eventually, he was out of the wooded stretch and into the open sunlit marsh again. A shadow sped across the water's surface. Matt looked up and saw an eagle balancing on air currents with its huge, fringed wings. He watched as it soared over the marsh. *Just like the one Quinn and I saw,* he remembered. *Only it hadn't come when Quinn was buried.* The thought made him sad. He dipped the oars into the water and began rowing again. Sweat ran down his face, and his shirt stuck to his back. Once again, he shipped the oars, this time to wipe his face. He was further down Herring Creek than he'd ever been before, but the channel seemed wider than Quinn had described it.

He rested for a moment, leaning against the oars. In the distance, the eagle was coasting in circles over the large hummock where the dead pine had stood. Then Matt looked again. It *couldn't* be! There was the old pine, its white trunk clearly silhouetted against the green backdrop of the hummock. *He must be imagining things,* he decided. He shielded his eyes with his hand. It was still there! He sat and thought for a moment. Maybe it was a mirage, like the kind Quinn used to talk about. "The heat plays tricks with your eyes," Quinn had said. People even saw things that weren't there.

Matt picked up the oars and started rowing again, hoping to find a better vantage point. He rowed fifty yards before stopping to look across the marsh. The eagle was still gliding lazily over the hummock. Matt stood up, balancing himself against the boat's rocking. He shaded his eyes with his hand and looked eastward. The white trunk was still there, pointing stiffly toward the sky.

Was he crazy? How could it be? Something tugged at the back of his mind, and he sat down, his thoughts darting first in one direction, then another. Suddenly, he knew what was wrong. The shape wasn't right! The trunk was too straight, too perfect for a tree, even for a pine tree. He looked again. Across the watery greenness, the old tree trunk took on a new and sinister form: a ship's mast, minus its sails. In a flash, Matt realized he was looking at the lone tall mast of the pirates' sloop!

Quinn had sent a message of help after all. And the eagle was his messenger.

Chapter
Twenty-two

When he finally did sleep,
Matt dreamed of a huge eagle circling
so low that he could see its fierce
yellow eyes. Then it slowly rose and
flew eastward over the marsh.

W hen Matt got back to Journey's End, Cato and Sam were cutting the grass in front of the house.

"Doctor? He went out on a 'mergency," Sam explained, leaning on the handle of his scythe.

Matt found Tom sharpening an ax blade behind a shed. His musket was propped against the woodpile.

"I thought you were fishing," he said when he saw Matt.

"I was," Matt replied. "When's your pa gittin' back?"

"I don't know. Said he had an emergency, and for me to stay close to the house."

Matt hesitated. He felt an overwhelming need to tell somebody what he had found. Tom bent over the ax head. Matt bit his lip and looked across the lawn, considering the advisability of confiding in Tom. After all, Tom had helped teach him how to shoot.

"I found the pirate boat," he said. The words hung suspended in the air, then burst like bubbles in the breeze.

"Where?" Tom asked, putting down his ax and staring at him.

"Hidden off Herrin' Crick," Matt said, gesturing across the marsh.

"How'd you find it?"

Tom listened intently as Matt described how first the pine tree was there and then it wasn't. Then this afternoon, it was back again.

Tom's blue eyes narrowed. "How can you be sure it's a mast?" he demanded.

"I'll show you."

"You know we can't leave when my father's not here," Tom said. But in spite of himself, he looked excited.

"After your pa gits back, we'll go see. Maybe you kin help me. There's got to be a way the sloop gits down the crick to its hidin' place, but there was nary a sign I could find."

"It'll be too late by the time he gets home." Tom's face fell.

"We'll go tomorrow then," said Matt. "If'n your pa says so."

Tom frowned and shook his head. "My pa?" he said. "He'd never let me go! He'll say it's too dangerous." Then his head shot up. "What if I tell him we're going fishing? If we take our poles, how would he know the difference?"

"Guess he wouldn't," Matt responded slowly.

"If it is the pirate ship you saw, and we can find out how to get to it, then it'll make it easier when the warship comes."

Matt nodded. He'd already thought of the same thing.

"Watch out!" Tom warned. Matt turned and saw Prudence coming toward them. "Meet me after supper," Tom whispered, "in the barn."

Twilight had almost faded into night when Tom slipped into the barn, where Matt was waiting for him. "Father said at supper that he's meeting with his tenant farmers tomorrow afternoon. That means he'll be home, so we can leave."

Matt's eyes lit up. "That's good," he said, "'cause then the tide will be low."

"What difference does that make?" Tom asked.

"I bin thinkin' on it ever since I got back from Herrin' Crick," Matt said. "The pirates must go in and out on the tide. If'n I'm right, the sloop will be in the same place as it were this afternoon. It won't be able to git out 'til the tide rises."

"I bet you're right!" Tom answered. "It'll be safe to explore, even though Father might not think so," he added. "We still best take our fishing gear."

Matt lay in bed that night, unable to sleep. The wind had risen, and a branch scratched against his window. First the whippoorwill, then the eagle, he thought. Would I have noticed the pine tree if I hadn't seen the eagle? Are the whippoorwill and the eagle really messengers from Quinn?

When he finally did sleep, Matt dreamed of a huge eagle circling so low that he could see its fierce yellow eyes. Then it slowly rose and flew eastward over the marsh.

Matt tried to run after it, but his legs wouldn't move. The eagle disappeared. Then he heard a whippoorwill calling. The sound came closer and closer.

Matt opened his eyes. He wasn't dreaming anymore. The sound of the whippoorwill carried into his room from the darkness outside. He got out of bed and went to the window. The moon, white and silent, was suspended over the marsh. It cast a silvery path across the water, up the slope, and to the house. The wind sighed, carrying a tang of salty air. The whippoorwill called again, its notes floating eerily through the shadows.

Chapter
Twenty-three

"There it be!" Matt said,
pointing eastward. In the distance,
a tall, slim form rose straight
upward from the hummock's
scrubby undergrowth.

Early in the afternoon, Dr. Campbell gave Matt and Tom permission to go fishing. Tom started rowing, heading the skiff toward the mouth of the creek. He threw his weight behind the oars, and the skiff moved rapidly downriver.

Before long, they entered Herring Creek. Last night's wind had died down; the creek was calm. The boat sliced through water that reflected an upside-down world of reeds and marshlands. Matt searched the shoreline. Everything looked normal. Thick clumps of oysters sprawled on the muddy flats. A white egret daintily stalked the water's edge.

"How far down the creek?" Tom asked.

"Not much further," Matt answered.

Tom hunched over the oars, stealing frequent glances over the marsh.

"I've never spent much time in boats," he confided. "I'm always busy around the farm."

Matt peered at the passing shoreline. "We should see it once't we round the next curve."

Tom dug the oars in harder. At the curve, he slowed down.

"There it be!" Matt said, pointing eastward. In the distance, a tall, slim form rose straight upward from the hummock's scrubby undergrowth.

"That's no tree trunk!" Tom exclaimed. He turned back toward Matt. "It's a ship's mast, all right." He looked eastward again. "It sure could fool you, though."

"We've got to find out how it gits back there!" Matt said.

Tom picked up the oars and began rowing again. They continued down the creek, carefully studying the shoreline for any signs of a waterway branching toward the hummock.

"Up ahead!" said Matt, pointing toward an opening farther along the bank. But when they drew closer, they saw that it was only a gut, blocked by a fallen tree. A wall of waving marsh grass, taller than both of them, framed each side of the stream, blocking their view of the hummock and mast.

"A ship couldn't get through there," Matt said, disappointed.

Tom continued rowing. Both boys anxiously scanned the bank as they threaded their way down the creek. Finally, the channel narrowed.

"It's no use!" Tom announced in disgust, slumping over the oars. "I'm tired of rowing," he added.

They exchanged places. Matt nosed the skiff around, heading back the way they'd come.

"Now I understand why they call you 'Water Rat,'" Tom said.

Matt clenched his fists around the oars and stared at Tom.

"I only meant it's easy to see that you know your way around boats and water," Tom added hastily.

Matt relaxed. "Pa showed me a lot 'fore he died."

Tom lapsed into silence. After a few moments, Matt said, "We've got to find out how the sloop gits back to that hummock!"

"Maybe there's a channel in from the bay," Tom suggested.

Matt didn't answer. Maybe Tom was right, he thought. But then why had the sloop been in Herring Creek that foggy afternoon? It didn't make sense.

"Hey! Wait a moment! Stop!" Tom cried.

"What's the matter?" Matt asked.

"I saw something shiny. Pull over."

Matt edged the skiff next to the shore, shipped the oars, and stepped onto the bank. The next second, the bank tilted, and he had to grab handfuls of tall marsh grass to keep from tumbling backward.

"What the devil?!" he exclaimed, fighting to regain his balance. He took a few steps forward and the ground tilted again. "Did you see that?" he asked. "Come here!"

Tom dropped the anchor and carefully stepped ashore. The bank tilted backward, and he fell into the muck. Matt reached down, giving Tom a hand. Tom scrambled to his feet. The ground tilted again.

"I'm going to find out what's going on!" Matt said, elbowing his way through the thick grass. The ground rocked gently. Matt carefully took a few more steps before turning back toward Tom.

"Come here!" he called, trying to keep his voice down. "Wait 'til you see what I found!"

Tom shoved his way through the tall grass and joined him. In front of them, a wide waterway lazily meandered toward the distant hummock.

"This has got to be the way the pirates come!" Matt said. "But how?" He turned quickly and again the earth tilted a little. The boys looked at each other, silent. Matt retraced his steps to the blocked gut. He began pulling on the fallen tree. With each tug, the ground rocked slightly. Suddenly, part of the tree came loose, toppling him backward. Matt scrambled to his feet, hauled harder, and pulled the huge branch from across the entrance to the gut. The ground rocked more violently, making Matt struggle to regain his balance. Only a stump remained on the opposite bank, bereft now of the huge limb that made it resemble a fallen tree.

"We've opened up a waterway, but it's still not big enough for a ship!" Tom said in frustration.

Matt studied the opening. Tom was right, but Matt was sure this was the way the pirates had come. It had to be. He paused to think. Quinn had forbidden him to go down Herring Creek, telling him it was silted in, but the creek was open; there wasn't any silt! Quinn hadn't wanted him to come down the creek because he must've known that it was the route the pirates took to reach their hiding place. Quinn had known it would be dangerous for Matt. That meant that the channel leading to the hummock had to branch off somewhere around here. This had to be the place! And the tilting ground—what did that have to do with it? There was something familiar about the motion.

Matt cautiously walked to the edge and dropped to his knees. Tom was gazing down the waterway. Matt thrust his arm into the water, fishing around under the surface.

"Wait a minute!" he said. "I think I got it!" A few minutes later, he hauled up several links of heavy chain. He gave a low whistle and turned to Tom. "I thought so! We're on a raft!" he exclaimed. "I figured that's why the ground rocked. Pa built me one when I was a tyke. The tiltin' felt just like that old raft!" He thrust his arm underwater again.

"I got it!" he said, rising to his feet. In his right hand he held part of a dripping chain. "When I put my hand in the water, I felt the wooden sidin'. Then I found the chain, but couldn't git it loose. But I just felt a hook and unfastened this end. Here, hold it," he said to Tom.

After Tom had inched over to Matt and taken the chain, Matt pulled the skiff over and retrieved the long pole. He stood up, shifted all his weight to his good leg, and shoved down with all his strength. The ground they were standing on slowly moved. Matt shoved downward again. This time, the land swung slowly away from the shoreline into the creek. They found themselves standing on a piece of earth about the size of the large carpet in the Campbells' parlor.

"How 'bout that!" Matt stated triumphantly. He dropped to his knees again and felt under the water. "Come here," he called. "I'll show you."

Tom crept carefully over to Matt and looked back at the creek's edge. Suddenly, he understood. Remove the tree limb from the bit of land they were standing on, and the channel entrance was wide enough for a sloop to pass through! A high tide would make it easy. He knelt down next to Matt.

"Run your hand underwater," Matt said.

Tom stuck an arm into the creek. Instantly, he felt the rough wooden siding. He looked at Matt, who was sitting back on his knees.

"I think I understand," Matt said slowly. "The pirates

built a great big raft and nailed on sides. Then they must've dug up chunks of marsh covered with growing grass and spread the chunks over the platform. It weighs the raft down 'nough so's the wooden part is underwater and the earth part with growing grass sticks out on top. They used good, stout timber so's it don't sink to the bottom—just low 'nough so's you can't see it. And the grass gets water, so's it grows. It probably didn't take long for the whole thing to look like it's always bin here!"

"They thought of everything," Tom said in amazement.

"The pirates go in and out on a high tide," Matt interrupted. "One of them must jump off'n the ship onto this side of the gut, pull away that big branch just like we did, unhook the chain, and pole the platform out into the crick. Then they sail their sloop through."

"That's got to be it!" Tom agreed, his voice rising in excitement.

"Then he poles the raft back," Matt continued, "hooks up the chain agin to keep it in place and shoves the big branch back into place. It would fool anybody—just like it done us! Then someone must throw him a line so he kin board ship agin."

They looked at each other for a second and grinned.

"Come on," said Matt. "Let's get it back into place."

Matt pulled the grass topped raft back to the shoreline so that it wedged neatly against the bank. Then he took the chain from Tom, knelt down and fumbled underwater until he had hooked it again. He straightened up and wiped the mud from his pants.

"Help me with the tree," he said.

The boys wrestled the huge branch back into place until the end rested against the stump. When they had finished, it looked as it had before—like a tree that had fallen over the entrance to the gut.

"Nobody'd ever guess!" said Matt.

"Hey! I forgot," said Tom. "The shiny thing I saw from the skiff."

He turned and shoved his way through the marsh grass while Matt waited. Tom returned a few minutes later.

"Look what I found!" he said, handing Matt a gold coin.

Matt turned it over in his hand. He had seen Eli with one in the tavern once. "Pirate gold!" he said, looking at Tom.

"I bet there're hundreds, maybe thousands, of these!" Tom cried.

They looked across the marsh to where the mast beckoned in the distance.

"When the warship comes, we'll be able to tell the cap'n where the pirates hide out," said Matt. "They'll git them!"

Tom laughed. "We'll be heroes!"

Matt hefted the coin in his hand. "Maybe Quash is back there," he said.

Tom shielded his eyes against the sun and looked toward the ship. "I hope so," he said quietly. Then he turned back toward the skiff. "Look!" he called in alarm.

Matt looked where Tom was pointing and instantly saw the cause of his fear. Incoming salt water was pouring under the fallen tree into the estuary beyond. In their excitement, they hadn't noticed that the tide had changed. He looked down the creek. The water was rising fast.

"Hurry!" Matt said. "We got to git away from here!"

Chapter Twenty-four

"It's amazing ye even found
the entrance. If one of the pirates
hadn't dropped a coin,
ye'd never have stopped."

It was late when they anchored the skiff at Journey's End and found Dr. Campbell in his office.

"We've found the pirates' hiding place, Father," Tom announced.

"Where?" his father demanded, rising to his feet.

Matt listened as Tom described how they'd been fishing in Herring Creek and spied a ship's mast in the distance. Tom carefully avoided telling his father how they'd planned the expedition the day before.

"They didn't see ye, did they?" the doctor interrupted.

"No," Matt replied, "but the tide was rising fast by the time we left."

Dr. Campbell gave a low whistle when they finished describing the concealed waterway. "That's about the cleverest thing I've heard of," he said. "It's amazing ye even found the entrance. If one of the pirates hadn't dropped a coin, ye'd never have stopped." He sat back in his chair and rubbed his chin.

"All right," he began. "I've heard that the warship has reached Appoquinimink. We must let the captain know that we've located the pirates. The sooner the warship gets here, the better!" He looked out the window and then back at the boys. "Tom," he said, "it's too late to start now, but first thing tomorrow morning, ye're to ride to Appoquinimink with a message I'll give ye for the captain."

Matt was milking the cows when Tom returned late the next afternoon. Matt saw immediately that he'd ridden Gypsy hard. Her head hung low, and her neck and withers were covered with dark sweat stains. Tom slid out of the saddle and leaned against the horse for a moment. Dr. Campbell came out of the house.

"I found the warship," Tom announced. "It's a big brig, all right!"

"And the captain?" his father asked.

"Captain Howard's his name. I gave him your message. He was very pleased with our news. He got out a chart and asked me to show him where the hideout is located. I showed him where Journey's End is, too."

"When's he coming?"

"Tomorrow. Captain Howard says he plans to get here just after nightfall. The brig is too big for a creek, so he'll anchor off the entrance and send in cutting-out parties."

"What are they?" Matt asked.

"He said armed sailors are loaded into small boats, like large rowboats, that can get down smaller waterways. The boats have cannons mounted on their prows."

"How will they find the hidden entrance?" Matt asked.

"He wants you and me to guide them," Tom answered, straightening his shoulders. "We're to meet them at Herring Creek, take them back to the blocked gut, and open up the hidden waterway. Then they'll raid the pirates."

A vast sense of relief washed over Matt. The nightmare was almost over. He looked at Dr. Campbell, who was standing near the mounting block.

"I'll not have ye two boys going by yourselves on such a mission," Dr. Campbell said sternly. "It's too dangerous!"

"Father!" Tom protested.

"Matt will go, as he knows the marsh better than anyone else. Since I want to confer with the captain, I'll go with him. I can give him a hand with opening the channel," Dr. Campbell continued. "But, Tom," he said, turning to his son, "ye'll have to stay here with the family."

"The captain said Matt and I were only to open the waterway, we weren't to go with them to where the pirate sloop is anchored," Tom pleaded. "And besides, you don't know how to open the channel, and I do!"

"No matter. I don't want ye going," Dr. Campbell said firmly. "We can't leave Mama, the baby, and your sisters here alone. It's the only sensible way, son. Besides, don't ye realize the service ye've already performed by riding all the way to Appoquinimink, finding the warship, and alerting Captain Howard? That was a job well done!"

"Well, I still think it would be better if I went, too," Tom insisted, but his face had brightened a little at his father's praise.

"All right, lads," Dr. Campbell said, turning toward the house. "Maria's got supper waiting for both of ye and then git off to bed. Tomorrow's a big day."

Matt was worried the next morning when he saw the overcast sky, but Dr. Campbell reassured him. "It will give the brig better cover on its way down the coast this evening," he said. "Now, I've got a lot of patients to see. Tom's saddling up for me, and Cato and Sam are working in the fields. I know waiting's the hard part," he said, laying a hand on Matt's shoulder, "but be patient. Tonight will come sooner than ye think." He slapped his riding crop against his leg. "I'll be just as glad as ye to see those devils behind bars!"

Instead of passing quickly, though, the hours seemed to drag. Matt was mucking out stalls in the barn when he went to the door to look outside. It had begun to drizzle. Picking up the pitchfork, he returned to work.

A short while later, Tom appeared, out of breath.

"There's a fence panel down along the road, and the horses have gotten out," he said. "I'll have to catch them!" He took a measure of corn, and grabbed a bridle and rope. "I'll be back as soon as I can. You stay close to the house," he instructed, hurrying out the door.

"Where's Tom?" Letty asked as soon as Matt came in for the noon meal. She listened as he explained about the runaway horses. "Are you telling me the truth?" she asked sharply. "He seemed awfully excited this morning."

Matt looked into her blue eyes. She stared back steadily. He shifted his weight onto his good leg. It was hard to fool her, but Tom really was chasing horses. "There's a fence panel down 'long the road," Matt explained. "If'n you don't believe me, go check it fer yourself!"

Letty's face flushed. "All right. I'm sorry. I believe you," she said.

Matt ate quickly and then left the kitchen, saying he had a lot of work to do. Carrying his musket, he walked down the drive toward the road. The drizzle had stopped, but the sky held the promise of more rain. The creek, a dull gray under the threatening sky, lay down the slope on his right. He took a few more strides and then suddenly stopped. A small boat had rounded the bend and was headed for the dock. Matt grasped the musket tighter. Without Tom and Dr. Campbell, he again was the only one left to protect Journey's End!

Chapter
Twenty-five

A figure stepped out and started
up the hill. Even at a distance,
there was something familiar about him.
Matt looked closer. It was Mingo!

M att backtracked up the drive, skirting the spring-house where Maria was working, and hid behind a clump of bushes. The boat tied up at the dock. A figure stepped out and started up the hill. Even at a distance, there was something familiar about him. Matt looked closer. It was Mingo!

Matt grabbed the slave by the arm. "Mingo, it's sure good to see you! What're you doin' here?"

"It's good to see you, too, boy. Yes, indeedy!" Mingo replied, but he didn't look happy. He looked upset.

"How'd you know where to find me?" Matt asked.

"I heard tell from Bessie. She told me ev'rybody at Sherburn is talkin' 'bout how you done hid the girls from the pirates. I sure was glad to hear you was safe. I bin missin' you." He frowned. "There's trouble, boy. Big trouble. That's why I come."

"What's wrong?"

"It's Eli. I'm sure he's in cahoots with them pirates."

"Eli and the pirates?" Matt said. "How do you know?" But already his mind was accepting what Mingo said. It was as if a giant piece of a puzzle fell into place.

"I hear things," Mingo said, looking around nervously. "The stranger, 'member who came that day Eli gave us the afternoon off? One I said looked like a fox?" Matt nodded. "Well, he's bin back a couple more times. Comes from downriver somewhere, and each time, Eli tells me to go fishin' and stay away 'til supper time.

"One night, I come back and Eli was passed out in the bar. I found the key, the one he wears 'round his neck, lying on the table. I unlocked the storeroom, and there were cases and cases of whiskey down there! I locked the door again, and put the key back so's he wouldn't know."

Matt's mind was racing ahead of Mingo's. Everyone knew that pirates were making it difficult for supply ships to reach the American shores. More pieces of the puzzle were falling into place.

"What I hear 'round the docks is that tavern owners is havin' trouble getting liquor 'cause of the pirates," Mingo continued. "Lots of folks who comes to the tavern says they come 'cause they can always count on Eli havin' anythin' they wants to drink. Seems to me that there stranger's a pirate, and he keeps ol' Eli supplied with whiskey."

In exchange, Eli supplies him with information, Matt thought. What better place than a waterfront bar to pick up news about cargoes and shipping? All Eli had to do was keep his ears open and pass on what he heard. The last piece of the puzzle clicked into place for Matt. Eli was a spy!

"Stranger's at the tavern right now," Mingo said. "Eli, he tole me to take the boat and go fishin'."

"Why'd you come here?" Matt asked.

"The whole town's bin talkin' 'bout how the government people's sendin' a warship down to ketch the pirates. Eli will be sure and warn the stranger, and they'll git away!"

He's right, but what did Mingo expect him to do, Matt wondered, looking into the slave's honest face.

"You could tell the doctor 'bout Eli," Mingo suggested as if he were reading Matt's mind. "That's why I come here—to tell you. Doc don't know me, but he'd listen to you! Maybe he kin do somethin'."

"He's away," Matt said.

Mingo's face fell. "What we goin' to do, then?" he asked. "That man won't stay at the tavern. Not after Eli tells him 'bout the warship. No, sir! Somebody's got to stop him from gittin' back to his ship! He'll go an' warn the other pirates, and they'll git away. Next thing you know, they'll raid 'nuther place and somebody may git killed!"

Matt thought quickly. Dr. Campbell hadn't said when he'd be back, and Tom could be chasing horses all afternoon. If anyone was going to stop the pirates, he would have to do it.

"I'll go, Mingo," Matt said.

"You?" Mingo asked in astonishment. "You only a boy!"

"I've got a musket, and I kin shoot."

"What will you do?"

"I'll think of somethin'," Matt said, sounding more confident than he felt.

"Ain't there nobody to help you?"

"No, but don't worry. Best thing fer you to do is to ketch some fish, go back, and act normal."

Mingo hesitated. He clearly didn't like the idea of leaving Matt to handle the job alone. But after Matt reassured him, Mingo reluctantly got into his boat and cast off.

"Where'd you git that boat?" Matt called after him.

"Eli got it after you left," Mingo answered, nosing it around so he was headed back down the creek. "You be keerful, boy! Hear?"

Matt didn't waste time. He found Sam. He told him that something had come up, and that he and Cato would have to stay near the house until either Tom or the doctor returned. Then he found Letty and motioned to her to follow him outside. Dr. Campbell had warned Tom and him not to alarm the family by saying they located the pirate ship, but there was no use keeping secrets from Letty now. He gave her a brief account about finding the pirates' hiding place and about Mingo's visit.

"If'n that man gits back to his ship, the pirates will escape on the next tide!" Matt said. "They'll keep on robbin' and killin'. And, sooner or later, they'll be back here fer your pa!"

"Oh, Matt," Letty said, biting her lip. "What will you do?"

"I don't know yet, but I'll do somethin'." It was the second time he'd made that promise without the slightest idea how he'd keep it.

"You should wait for Papa and Tom," Letty told him.

"I can't. I'd miss the pirate on his way back to his ship.

Tell your pa and Tom what happened. Say I'll be back soon's I can. And Letty, go to your pa's office and bring me his musket and powder horn. I'll be down at the dock."

Letty turned and fled into the house. Matt returned to the dock and put his musket and powderhorn under the seat in the skiff. He was inserting the oarlocks when she came hurrying toward him.

"Here's Papa's gun and powderhorn," she said, reaching over to hand them to him. Matt placed them next to his own musket and pushed away from the dock. Letty watched, a distressed look on her face. Matt lifted a hand in farewell and began rowing. Just before rounding the bend, he glanced over his shoulder. Letty was still watching, a lonely figure dressed in blue gingham, perched at the end of the dock.

Matt navigated the skiff out of the creek and headed upriver. He had no idea how he was going to do it, but somehow he was going to have to intercept the pirate. He rowed steadily, considering and rejecting one plan after another. His one real advantage, Matt sensed, was surprise.

He'd gone about a mile when he spied a point of land jutting into the river. It offered as good a place as any for an ambush. He slid the prow of the boat into the thick reeds at the water's edge and shipped his oars.

The river was narrow here, and a boat would be forced to pass close to his hiding place. He primed and loaded both muskets and laid them lengthwise across the seat. It began drizzling again. The gray river, the gray sky, and the drizzle merged into a single, depressing landscape stretching as far as Matt could see.

The only way to stop the pirate, Matt decided, would be to shoot him. He'd never shot anybody in his life. Never even aimed a gun at anyone. What would it be like to sight down the barrel at another human being? Could he squeeze the trigger? Mingo was right. This wasn't a job for a boy. With each passing moment, Matt felt a little more of his courage draining away.

Then, all of a sudden, a small sailboat, scarcely bigger than his own skiff, rounded the point. Matt tensed, studying the man at the tiller. There was no mistaking the long, weasel-like face with the drooping mustache. Matt's heart began beating faster. He picked up his musket and cradled it against his shoulder, the way Tom had taught him. He sighted down the barrel. If only Tom were here now! The man's head came into view. Matt's hand was shaking badly. He took a deep breath to steady himself. He couldn't do it, Matt realized. He couldn't pull the trigger! In that instant, the man passed out of view. How can I be such a fool, Matt immediately thought.

He remembered Quinn lying in the marsh with a bullet hole in his head. If the pirate gets away, he'll warn the others, and they'll escape, Matt told himself. The robbing and killing will go on. What if I shoot only to injure the pirate? What if I don't kill him but hurt him enough so he can't get back to his sloop?

The boat sailed into view again. Matt took another deep breath, sighted down the barrel, and squeezed the trigger. There was an explosion, followed by a dull thud. He had hit the boat! The man at the tiller jerked around. Matt grabbed the other musket and sighted again. This time he aimed below the boat's waterline on purpose. Maybe he could sink the boat. He squeezed the trigger, and a bullet streaked across the water. It too thwacked the pirate's boat. He was dimly aware that the pirate had grabbed a rifle. Matt ducked and began to reload. A shot rang out, but the pirate's bullet plowed harmlessly into the muddy bank behind Matt. Now the pirate had to reload. Matt straightened up again, sighted, and pulled the trigger. Again, there was a satisfying thwack as his bullet hit the pirate's boat.

Matt reached for the other musket. Out of the corner of his eye, he saw the pirate aiming his rifle in his direction. Then, suddenly, a gust of wind caught the sail on the other boat and swung the boom around sharply, catching the pirate on the back of his shoulders. The rifle flew out of his hands. Now Matt had the advantage. He reloaded and aimed. This time, the bullet splintered the stern of the pirate's boat. The pirate cursed loudly. Matt reloaded and aimed again. He pulled the trigger, and a gaping hole appeared in the stern. The pirate's boat began listing. Matt watched him scurry about his sailboat, trying to stanch the flow of water. The man paused once to shake his fist at Matt. His boat was listing badly now. Finally, the pirate abandoned efforts to stop the flooding. He scrambled toward the bow. Within minutes, the stern disappeared underwater, and the boat began sinking. A few minutes later, the pirate jumped overboard and struggled toward the opposite shore.

Matt watched him clamber up the muddy bank. He glanced at Matt. Matt rose to his feet and pointed his empty musket at him. The pirate let out a howl of fear and stumbled out of sight, into the marsh. Matt lowered the musket. He had done it! There was no way now that the man could warn the others. It wasn't until he sat down again that Matt realized that he was shaking.

Chapter
Twenty-six

Letty was waiting for him when
he returned. "Did you get him?"
she asked eagerly, helping him
fasten the bow line.

L etty was waiting for him when he returned. "Did you get him?" she asked eagerly, helping him fasten the bow line.

"No," Matt replied, "but I sank his boat!"

"Then he can't warn the others?"

"That's right," Matt said. "Did you tell your pa that I left the place today?"

She shook her head. "I didn't have time to because—" she began.

"Good," Matt interrupted, "he might've bin mad at me." Then he began laughing. "You should've seen that pirate when he reached shore! I pointed my musket at him, and you n'ver did hear sich a holler. And my musket was empty!"

Letty clapped her hands. Matt felt a warm glow at the sight of her smiling face. Then her smile vanished. "Tom's hurt!" she said.

"What happened?"

"The horses nearly got to Sherburn before he caught them. He rode Gypsy home bareback and led Gray Fox, but something spooked Gypsy near our drive, and she suddenly reared. Tom had a bad fall. Sam and Cato found him and got him to the house. Father's taking care of him now."

"Is he hurt bad?"

"His shoulder's broken. I don't know what else."

"Kin I see him?" Matt asked. He hoped Tom wasn't hurt as badly as Letty seemed to think. It was strange how the antagonism between Tom and Matt had completely evaporated over the past few weeks.

They hurried up the hill as fast as Matt could manage. He listened absent-mindedly to Letty's chatter—half of him was paying attention, the other half casting ahead to the coming evening and the rendezvous with the warship.

He paused at the threshold of Tom's room. Tom was worse than Matt had expected. He lay on his back, his eyes closed, pale as the sheet he lay on. Dr. Campbell was knotting a bandage around his shoulder.

"He's unconscious," the doctor said, turning from the bed when he saw Matt. "He's smashed his shoulder badly. Broke his collarbone too. The real worry now is his concussion. I'll have to watch him carefully through the night."

Matt's eyes met the doctor's. It was plain he was worried about Tom.

"I haven't forgotten about the warship," Dr. Campbell said quietly, "but I can't leave Tom."

Matt looked at him. This was a fine fix, he realized.

"We'll talk later in my office," Dr. Campbell continued. He bent over Tom, pulled open an eyelid, and peered into his eye.

No point in bothering the doctor about what had happened this afternoon, Matt decided. Besides, he wouldn't like Matt's having left the farm with only Cato and Sam to guard the family. Matt stole a last look at Tom before going up to his room and collapsing on the bed. Was Tom going to be all right? What was a "concussion," at any rate?

Matt closed his eyes, but he couldn't sleep. He tossed and turned, thinking about the evening ahead. It was too late to change plans now. The warship was already on its way. Could he open the channel by himself? In the dark? He sighed and rolled over. He had to get some rest before taking the boat out again.

When Maria rang the dinner bell, Matt went downstairs. The moist, yeasty smell of freshly baked bread filled the kitchen, but he wasn't hungry. To make matters worse, it had started raining again. The conversation at the kitchen table revolved around Tom's accident. A soon as he could, Matt left and went to the doctor's office. As he walked down the hall, he heard Letty playing the pianoforte in the parlor.

"Letty just told me a few moments ago that ye stopped one of the pirates this afternoon," Dr. Campbell said as soon as he saw Matt. "What happened?"

Matt cleared his throat and described Mingo's visit.

"I didn't want the pirate to git back to his ship and warn the others," he said. He explained how he'd taken the muskets and skiff and had ambushed the boat.

Dr. Campbell listened attentively. "Well done, lad!" he said when Matt finished.

Matt was relieved. Dr. Campbell didn't seem angry that he'd left Journey's End. "So Eli's a spy?" the doctor asked.

"Mingo says so," Matt replied. "I reckon he's right."

Dr. Campbell sat quietly for a moment. "A spy and a thief," he said. "Rotten to the core. He should be behind bars!"

For a moment, Matt was speechless. Eli a prisoner? Locked up? The tables had suddenly turned! If Eli was arrested, all Matt's worries about the robbery, Mr. Barrett, and Eli would be over. Matt's future suddenly seemed a lot brighter. He pictured Eli's ham-like fists shaking the cell bars, and he tucked the vision into the back of his mind, to be pulled out later and savored.

"I don't think ye should go alone this evening," the doctor advised, interrupting Matt's thoughts. "But I can't leave Tom, and Cato would be useless. He's terrified of boats and water."

"But," Matt protested, "what happens to the warship? It's on the way! They can't find the waterway without me."

Dr. Campbell frowned, drumming his fingers on his desk. "I can't forbid ye, ye're not my son," he said. "But I don't like it. It's too dangerous!"

"I can do it! I know I can!" Matt insisted, squaring his shoulders.

The doctor glanced out the window. "The rain's stopped. That's one good sign," he said.

"I'll be keerful," Matt pleaded.

Dr. Campbell sighed. "All right," he finally agreed. "But, mind ye, ye're only to open the channel for the British. Don't go any farther than the entrance!"

"I promise," Matt replied.

He was walking down the hall when Letty suddenly appeared in the parlor doorway. "I heard Papa say you could go," she said, worried.

"You've bin listenin' to what goes on in your pa's office agin," Matt remarked.

"Oh, Matt," Letty exclaimed, ignoring what he'd said. "Don't go. It's dangerous!"

"I'll be all right," Matt told her, but inside he felt a twinge of fear.

"I'll go with you!" she declared.

"You?" He gaped at her.

Her face flushed. "I could help you," she said quietly.

For a moment, Matt was speechless. Then he collected his wits. "You can't go," he mumbled. "It ain't fitten fer a girl!"

He turned abruptly toward the kitchen, afraid for her to see his face. She cared, he marveled. She'd offered to help! And Dr. Campbell cared too, or he wouldn't be worried. The emptiness and loneliness that had been part of him ever since Pa died began to slowly dissolve.

Chapter
Twenty-seven

Behind him, it seemed as though
dozens of pairs of oars flashed into the
water at once. They turned into the
creek, Matt's skiff leading the way.

Evening was fast approaching as Matt crossed the lawn and headed down the slope. The rain had stopped, but a land breeze had come up, blowing eastward across the marsh to the bay. Matt climbed into the skiff and stashed the musket, powder, and shot under the seat. For the second time that day he cast off and began rowing, trying not to worry about what lay ahead. It was too late for worrying now, at any rate. The die was already cast.

Once out of the protection of the creek, Matt found that the wind was stronger. He had to work harder to keep the skiff on course. Clouds obscured the sky. Twilight had faded into an early nightfall by the time he approached Herring Creek. He peered through the gathering darkness. Then, emerging from the gloom, Matt saw the outline of a large ship beyond the next point. He threw all his weight into the oars until the skiff bounced through the water, wetting him with spray.

When he pulled abreast of the warship, Matt stopped and shipped the oars. Cupping his hands around his mouth, he called out, "Ahoy, there!"

From somewhere above, a small light blinked and was just as quickly extinguished.

"Be ye a Campbell from Journey's End?" a voice called softly into the night.

"No, but Dr. Campbell sent me," Matt replied. "His boy's hurt bad, so he couldn't come."

"Just a minute."

A moment later, another voice called out. "This is Captain Howard speaking. Take yer skiff toward the stern, and tie up at the steps."

"Yes, sir," Matt answered. When he reached the steps, he fastened the line.

A grate slid open in the bulwarks. A minute later, a figure began climbing down the wooden ladder attached to the vessel's side.

"Make way!" the captain said.

Matt held on to the narrow stairs while the captain stepped down into the skiff. When it had stopped rocking, Captain Howard inched his way toward the stern seat. He spread out his long, dark, swallowtailed coat before he sat down.

"Head toward the point," he instructed Matt. "There's a small cover just beyond it where my men are waiting in boats. As ye are to lead us, I want to be in yer boat."

Matt began rowing in the direction the captain had indicated.

"What happened to the Campbells?" the captain inquired. He spoke in a strange, clipped manner.

"That's a stroke of bad luck," he said when Matt finished describing Tom's accident. "Do ye think ye can find this place on yer own?"

"Yes, sir," Matt replied in as confident a voice as he could muster.

As they neared land, a boat much longer than the skiff, and shaped like an oversized rowboat, pulled out of the shadows. A torch flared. Matt saw three identical boats filled with British sailors armed with muskets and swords. A small cannon was mounted on the prow of each boat.

"Put out that torch, ye fool!" Captain Howard ordered.

The light was doused, and night closed in again.

"All right, men," the captain said. "We're going up the creek. I'll stay with the boy and you follow. Keep quiet and no more lights!"

Matt began rowing. Behind him, it seemed as though dozens of pairs of oars flashed into the water at once. They turned into the creek, Matt's skiff leading the way.

"Where is the pirates' lair?" the captain asked.

After listening to Matt's description, he grunted and said, "No wonder nobody's been able to find those blackguards!" He sat erect, scanning the passing shoreline.

"There be somethin' else Dr. Campbell says I should tell you," Matt began nervously. "There be a tavern keeper in Fast Landin' by the name of Eli. He's a spy!"

The captain's head swiveled in Matt's direction. "How do ye know?"

"He finds out what ships will be sailing, and then he sends messages to the pirates."

"What proof do ye have?" Captain Howard asked.

"Only what Mingo says, but Dr. Campbell and me, we reckon Mingo's right. He'd know 'cause he works all day with Eli. He sees all what goes on." In a low voice, Matt described the comings and goings of the stranger, followed by the arrival of caseloads of whiskey. He also discussed Eli's unusual behavior whenever the stranger appeared at the tavern.

"A bartender in a port tavern. A perfect opportunity for hearing news of shipping!" the captain snapped when Matt had finished. "We'll have to take him into custody for questioning."

There it was again! Eli was going to be arrested. Matt suppressed a thrill of anticipation. He looked over his shoulder. The British boats were strung out behind him. The only noise came from the dipping of oars into the water.

"How far ahead is this channel?" the captain asked.

"Not much farther," Matt replied.

Matt studied the shoreline carefully. He knew he mustn't miss the entrance. A few minutes later, he spotted the blurred shape of a fallen tree. As they drew nearer, he saw it spanned a small stream.

"This be it," he whispered.

"It hardly seems possible," the captain said, eyeing the gut straddled by the fallen tree.

"You'll see," Matt told him, nosing the skiff against the bank and dropping anchor. The captain stood up and called out quietly to the nearest boat.

"Halt! Pass the word."

Matt found the long pole and carefully stepped onto the marshy bank. The ground tilted and then righted itself. He jabbed the pole into the ground for support. All around him lay the marsh, dark and mysterious. Now came the hard part, he thought to himself. Would he be able to open the channel by himself? If only Tom were here!

He cautiously made his way to where the fallen limb blocked the gut. He had forgotten how big it was. Grabbing a branch, he started pulling. It barely moved. Maybe he wouldn't be able to do it. Maybe it'd only worked last time because it was daylight and he could see what he was doing. He dug his feet into the mud and pulled with all his strength. The branch gave a little. He braced himself and pulled again. Gradually, the branch yielded until Matt finally hauled it clear of the water.

"Do ye need help?" the captain asked in a low voice.

"No, sir," Matt answered. He knelt down and began fumbling underwater. What if he couldn't find the chain, he worried. He was aware of Captain Howard watching him from the skiff. And beyond the captain, Matt felt the eyes of the waiting sailors upon him. What if he had brought them all this distance and then wasn't able to open the channel? He thrust his arms deeper into the water. Where was the chain? Then, finally, he felt the cold metal links. He grabbed hold and yanked. The chain came free. With a vast sense of relief, Matt stood up and hooked it to a branch of the tree trunk.

When he had made sure the chain was securely fastened, Matt retrieved the long pole and shoved it down into the water. Nothing happened. But when he pushed harder, the "ground" slowly began to swing into the creek. He carefully worked it away from the shoreline and out of the way of the waiting boats, playing out the chain as needed.

"I'll be confounded!" the captain said, as the channel's true width was revealed.

Matt straightened up and called to the captain in a low

voice. "You'll be findin' the pirate ship a couple hundred yards down this little crick."

The captain called softly for the nearest boat to come alongside. With the help of one of his men, he transferred from the skiff to the British boat. Then he signaled the other boats to line up behind.

"Battle positions, men," he ordered in a low voice. "Follow me."

Matt stood silently as the small convoy swept past him and out of sight down the channel. When the last boat disappeared, he poled the overgrown, oversized raft closer to shore and peered down the channel into darkness. Nothing. The minutes passed slowly. Then, from somewhere in the murky darkness surrounding him, came a whippoorwill's cry. The whippoorwill called again, its forlorn notes hovering on the night air. Matt shivered. It was as if Quinn's spirit were somewhere nearby, watching and waiting. Maybe capturing the pirates was the unfinished business that wouldn't let Quinn's spirit rest, he thought.

Matt shifted restlessly. A fish jumped in the water, leaving a ghostly trail of phosphorescent bubbles. Matt stared in the direction of the hummock, but there was only blackness. Another minute passed. Then five more.

Suddenly, an explosion ripped the silence. Matt jumped as a second and then a third blast followed. Only cannons could make that much noise! Matt moved as far forward on the makeshift raft as he dared, struggling to keep his balance as the ground rocked underneath. He found it unbearable not to see what was happening. He grabbed the pole and shoved hard, wedging the raft against the bank. He stepped ashore. A small tree, its gnarled, windswept branches twisting low to the ground, loomed ahead. Matt carefully picked his way over the marshy ground and, grabbing a branch, pulled himself up. Then, reaching for another branch, he climbed up high enough so he could see down the channel.

The cannons boomed again, echoing across the marsh. It seemed to Matt as if a thousand birds squawked in protest. In the short flash of light from the cannon's explosion, Matt saw the pirate ship surrounded by the smaller boats of the Royal Navy. Silhouetted against the blackness, pirates dashed from one side of their sloop to the other. The staccato popping of musket fire punctuated the night. As the bursts of light blazed across the horizon, Matt saw men from the Royal Navy swarm up the sides of the pirate ship.

It was difficult to follow the battle from such a distance. Matt gripped the tree trunk tighter. He stared down the channel, his heart hammering. With the cannons, the gunfire, and the birds, it seemed to him that the whole marsh was in an uproar. The cannons rumbled again. Matt saw that the sailors had boarded the sloop. Another salvo of musket fire splintered the darkness. Matt caught the glint of saber against saber, as the pirates fought desperately to protect their ship from the British forces.

Then the cannons roared once more, followed by an explosion that lit up the marsh. Before blackness enveloped the scene again, Matt saw more sailors swarming up the sides of the pirate vessel. Another explosion rent the air. The shouting grew louder. Then the cannons fell silent.

Matt listened intently. Minutes dragged by. The shouts grew fewer. Had the British captured the pirates? Gradually, silence returned to the marsh, interrupted only by an occasional shout. Matt climbed down stiffly from the tree and made his way back to the raft. What if the pirates had beaten back the British? The British outnumbered them, but the pirates had the bigger boat. He shivered again. It must be nerves.

He heard a sound again and cocked his head. Something was splashing. A boat was coming up the channel! He crouched down behind a clump of marsh grass and waited. What if it was the pirate ship, he fretted. His skin prickled at the thought. Less than a minute later, he saw the shadowy outline of a boat emerging from the darkness. He strained his eyes. Yes! There it was! A cannon was mounted on the bow. It was a British boat!

He stood up quickly and hollered, "Over here!"

A torch was lit, and, as the boat drew nearer, Matt saw a group of rough-looking, bearded men sitting midship, surrounded by armed British sailors. Several of the pirates and one of the British were wounded.

"There are more coming," a British sailor called to Matt as the boat passed out of the channel and into the creek. Another boat followed shortly, loaded with more armed sailors guarding silent captives. A third boat appeared. Several of the crew brandished torches.

"Captain's aboard the pirate ship," an officer called to Matt, "but he says to tell ye that ye have his thanks for yer help tonight. He says ye're to go home now."

As the boat drew abreast, Matt studied the faces of the pirates in the flickering torchlight. They stared back sullenly. Several looked familiar. Then one of them, partially hidden by the press of bodies, rose to his feet. Blood seeped from a shoulder wound. Matt looked at him carefully. There was no mistaking the scar running down the left side of his face. The pirate captain leaned toward Matt and spat.

Chapter
Twenty-eight

For a second, it was last night again.
Matt saw the pirate captain, the red scar
more vivid than ever in the torchlight,
stand in the boat and spit at him.

att looked at the marsh shimmering in the summer sun. The tall grass swayed in the breeze as sea gulls, searching for food, glided on air currents. Nothing had changed. It was hard to believe that last night had ever happened.

Morning turned into noon and then slowly became afternoon. Matt alternated between working halfheartedly in the vegetable garden and anxiously checking the drive for signs of Sheriff Evans. Once, he snuck into the house and crept up the stairs to see Tom, but the door to his room was closed, so Matt went outside again.

Late that afternoon, when the breeze had died down and the song of the crickets rose into the air, Letty called out, "Matt! Matt! Come quickly!"

Matt dropped the hoe, wiped his face with his sleeve, and went around to the front of the house.

"Captain Howard's inside!"

Matt's face lit up. Now he could find out what had happened to the pirates!

Captain Howard, dressed in white britches and a swallowtailed Royal Navy coat, stood in the center of the parlor. His boots were shinier than any Matt had ever seen, shinier even than Mr. Barrett's. On his head he wore a stiff-looking tricorn hat. Another officer stood several paces behind him. Tom, pale but alert, lay on the sofa. He smiled wanly at Matt. Mrs. Campbell sat next to her son.

"Yes," Dr. Campbell was saying, "our son is better, but he must stay quiet."

"I'm glad he's improving," the captain said, breaking off as Letty and Matt entered the room. "Here's the lad that showed me the hidden waterway last night!" he said, extending a hand toward Matt.

All of a sudden, Matt was conscious of his own dirty, calloused hands. He furtively wiped them on his pants.

"Ye did a fine job guiding us through the marsh last evening," Captain Howard said.

"Where're the pirates now?" Matt wanted to know.

"Locked up belowdecks on my ship," the captain responded. "And a rougher, more disreputable-looking bunch I've never seen!"

"Can you tell us what happened?" Dr. Campbell asked.

"Gladly!" the captain answered. "We took them by surprise on their ship. They were preparing to go out on the tide. We had quite a battle before we were able to overcome them."

"We could even hear the cannons at Journey's End," Mrs. Campbell interjected.

"But with four boats," Captain Howard continued, "we were able to surround their sloop and fire from all sides. Even so, for a few moments I had my doubts about the outcome. But I've a good crew and they held steady and, finally, we were able to capture the devils!"

"What kind of ship did they have?" Dr. Campbell asked. "Matt said it was strange to him."

"It's a new type of boat called a Jamaica sloop. Small and built for speed, with a low freeboard and long bow."

"Perfect for pirates!" Dr. Campbell said.

"Exactly," the captain agreed. Turning back to Matt, he said, "They had a regular settlement on that hummock. There were a couple of shacks, some outfitted with bunks and two others filled with loot. Every sort of thing you can imagine: foodstuffs, jewelry, cases of whiskey—"

"Gold?" Matt interrupted.

"Yes, gold, too," Captain Howard confirmed. "Taken from ships they'd plundered. My senior officer is tallying it right now."

"I told you there'd be lots of gold," Tom said in a weak voice.

"We found a large cache of arms and ammunition. Even some black powder," Captain Howard went on. "With their arms supplies, the pirates were in a position to terrorize the entire coast. Ye've performed a great service by locating their hideaway." He signaled to his officer, who came forward to hand him two pistols.

"These belonged to the pirate captain," Captain Howard said, turning back to Matt. "I want ye to have them as a reminder of the service ye gave the Royal Navy in finding the pirates' hideout."

Matt shifted his weight onto his good leg. Once again he was the focus of attention, just like last night when he returned to Journey's End and had found everyone waiting up for him. He stepped up to the captain and took the pistols.

"Thank you, sir!" he said, hefting them in his hands. He hesitated a moment. It seemed as good a time as any to ask the question that was preying on his mind. "Did you tell Sheriff Evans 'bout Eli, the tavern keeper?" Matt held his breath.

"I sent word to Sheriff Evans earlier today to immediately question this Eli. I also told him to bring Eli out here this afternoon so I can have a look at him."

Matt exhaled a long, slow breath. His mind was no longer focused on the pirates. It had raced forward to Fast Landing. If the sheriff had gotten Eli to confess, then the long nightmare—the beatings, being forced to run for his life, all the worrying and uncertainty—would finally be over. An incredible feeling of lightness washed over him.

"What about Quash, our man they took from here?" Mrs. Campbell asked.

"He was one of several poor souls we found wandering around," Captain Howard replied. "I told them they'd be released when I returned to the ship this afternoon. He should be back here with you by this evening."

"Poor Quash! I'll be so happy to see him!" Letty said.

Suddenly, the sound of angry voices came from outside. Everyone turned as the front door burst open. Matt froze when he saw Sheriff Evans, followed by Eli in the custody of two deputies. As they entered the room, Eli glared at Matt.

Matt's legs trembled. For a moment, it was as if he were back at the tavern, facing Eli alone. Fear coursed through him. He gripped the back of a chair to steady himself.

"Have you questioned your prisoner, Sheriff?" Captain Howard demanded.

Matt relaxed. Captain Howard and his aide were here. So were Dr. Campbell and the sheriff. Eli couldn't hurt him, he realized. The deputies held Eli, his arms firmly pinioned behind his back.

"I have, sir," Sheriff Evans told the captain. "And he's guilty, all right. It took me and my men a bit of time to get at the truth, but we finally got it. You were right—he's a spy!"

So it was true! Matt looked around the room, but all eyes were fastened intently on Eli.

"Admitted he'd been doing business with the pirates for a long while," the sheriff continued. "Sending shipping news in exchange for all the whiskey he needed for his tavern. Told us they sometimes even paid him in gold."

For a moment the room was silent. Then Dr. Campbell exclaimed, "A traitor in our midst all these years!"

"And he'll be lucky he doesn't hang for his treason!" Captain Howard added. "At the very least, he'll be serving a long jail sentence."

Matt stood stock still, scarcely able to comprehend what he'd heard. He looked at Eli and saw that the tavern keeper's normally red face was pale.

"Ye've done a good job, Sheriff," Captain Howard said. "Now, if the doctor will let you borrow his sloop so ye have a way to get back, I'd like ye to take this man out to my ship and turn him over to the custody of Lieutenant Tanner."

He turned back to the others. "I'm setting sail shortly for Philadelphia," he said, motioning his officer to get ready to go. "Once there, I'll turn the pirates and the spy over to the proper authorities."

Leave? The captain was leaving! Matt glanced at Eli again and collected his wits. "Captain, did the sheriff talk to you 'bout a Mr. Barrett?" he asked, scarcely recognizing his own voice.

Eli blinked but remained silent. Matt waited with bated breath, aware that everyone was watching him. Letty stared at him with eyes that seemed twice their normal size.

"Tarnation! I clean forgot the robbery what with all this pirate business," Sheriff Evans exclaimed. He looked at Eli. "That was another one of your dirty doings, wasn't it?"

Eli raised his head. "I didn't rob nobody. 'Twas the lad over there who done it," he accused, nodding in Matt's direction.

Suddenly all the beatings and all the years of meanness and drudgery at Eli's hands rose up and confronted Matt. "Liar! Liar!" he yelled. "I seen you do it with my own two eyes!"

Eli's eyes narrowed. "The boy done it!" he said. "I know he done it 'cause he run away afterward. Clean disappeared!"

"I was watching through the window—" Matt began.

"That's part of your trouble," Eli interrupted savagely. "Snooping! Always spying on people! Well, this time the table's turned on you. I seen you take the gold out of Barrett's waistcoat and pad his money bag with your fishing sinkers!"

"How'd you know lead sinkers were in the money bag?" Matt asked in a dangerously quiet voice.

Eli's face twisted in confusion. His gaze darted nervously around the room. Then he collected himself. "'Cause I seen you do it. I seen you!" he asserted.

A red-hot rage overwhelmed Matt. He started across the room toward the tavern keeper. He found himself directly in front of Eli. The deputies tightened their grip on Eli's arms until he winced.

"Tell them how you got Mr. Barrett so drunk, he passed

out so you could rob him!" he shouted, his eyes blazing with fury.

Eli flinched. For a moment his eyes wavered.

Matt pressed closer. "Tell the truth!" he shouted. "'Cause Mr. Barrett's comin' back, and if'n you don't own up, he'll tell what really happened when he gits here!"

"Ha!" Eli retorted, on the offensive again. "I seen you run across the yard and into the woods, leaving poor Barrett passed out on the floor, his pockets inside out and empty 'cause you took his money!"

"Then how come you didn't help him? You jist let him git up, never said nuthin', nary a word 'bout his havin' been robbed. Even when he left the tavern you just let him go on his way," Matt shot back. "I'll tell you why," he continued, "'cause you're lyin'. You didn't do nuthin' 'cause you didn't want him to find out that he'd been robbed 'til he was a long ways from the tavern."

Sheriff Evans let out a whistle. "By golly, the lad's made a good point!" he exclaimed.

Suddenly, fear replaced the belligerence on Eli's face. He lowered his head. He realized he'd trapped himself. "I didn't hurt him none," he whined. "Just took the money."

Matt took a deep breath to steady himself. The words he'd been waiting so long to hear had finally been said. Now, no one could think him guilty any longer. Letty clapped her hands and beamed.

"Well, we've got a roomful of witnesses to that confession!" Captain Howard said, breaking the silence. "I'll be sure to add robbery to his list of crimes when I turn him over to the authorities. And now, we really must leave if we're to reach Philadelphia by morning." He shook hands with Dr. Campbell and departed, followed by his officer.

The sheriff paused in front of Matt. "You've not had an easy time, my boy," he said kindly, "living with that brute." Then he and his deputies, with Eli firmly between them, followed the captain out.

As they neared the door, Eli turned his head toward Matt and snarled, "When I think of all I done for you the past four years!"

Suddenly, Mrs. Campbell leaped to her feet. "What have you ever done for this boy except keep him captive and make him work day and night?" she demanded in a shaking voice. Matt stared at Mrs. Campbell in amazement. Her small frame was trembling with anger.

"We're going to see Matt gets an education," she stated firmly. "We're going to give him a chance to make a decent life for himself!"

Eli scowled at her unexpected defense of Matt, but before he could answer, the deputies hustled him out of the room.

Matt sank into a chair near Letty. A lump formed in his throat. He tried to speak but couldn't. Through the window he saw Eli being led across the lawn toward the creek.

Then his thoughts darted back to the tavern. He saw Eli's red face glaring at him. He saw himself, terrified, running away from Eli the night of the storm. His thoughts next flashed to Quinn. Quinn! Matt saw the Indian's face staring blankly up at him from the muddy creek bank, the third eye in his forehead encrusted with dried blood.

For a second, it was last night again. Matt saw the pirate captain, the red scar more vivid than ever in the torchlight, stand in the boat and spit at him. Then Matt's thoughts flashed back to Journey's End and to all the problems of his first weeks here.

He looked around the room at the faces that had become so familiar to him. Mrs. Campbell and the doctor were smiling at him. Tom was grinning broadly. Letty was still smiling, too. Odd, he thought, he'd never noticed before how an inner light seemed to shine from Letty's eyes when she was happy. And then, from somewhere deep within himself, sprang the overwhelming conviction that here, at Journey's End, with the Campbells, he had found his own journey's end, too.

MONTGOMERY COUNTY-NORRISTOWN PUBLIC LIBRARY
NORRISTOWN. PA 19401

Text copyright © 1998 by Marnie Laird
Illustrations copyright © 1998 by Andrea Shine
All rights reserved
Library of Congress catalog card number: 97-62305
Printed in the United States of America
Designed by Bretton Clark
First edition, 1998

J LAI 731311
Laird, Marnie.
Water rat

DISCARDED
LIST A
NORRISTOWN, MDE & LIBRARY